The Wind Thief

By Martha Engber

For information contact:
ALONDRA PRESS PUBLISHING COMPANY
Houston, Texas 77043
lark@alondrapress.com
www.alondrapress.com

ISBN 978-0-9814523-4-0

Library of Congress Control Number 2009934590

Printed in the United States of America

Cover design: AlphaGraphics of Houston, TX
Editor: Penelope Aletras-Leight

The Wind Thief

by Martha Engber

WWW.ALONDRAPRESS.COM

Dedication

To Mike

Two can do what is impossible for one.
— Arab proverb

Acknowledgments

Special thanks are owed to Alan Tracey and Dennis Side, two dogged devotees of writing and great literature. I would also like to thank Charlotte Cook, Edie Matthews, Claudia Arndt and every member of the Monday Night Writers who offered input.

THE WIND THIEF

Part I

Marhaba.

Hello.

CHAPTER 1
Algeria

Ajay turned his face to the burning sun, and smiled. Because really, how funny. To escape Algiers only to become lost by way of this desolate road in the Sahara Desert and so meet danger once again. Like running into someone he'd cheated.

But the smile was brief and ephemeral. He'd survived nineteen orphaned years on this rabid earth — nineteen more than anyone could have expected — only to face death now. Well, he wouldn't do it, wouldn't die. Because he had someplace to go. Someplace he was long overdue and had traveled too far from Mumbai to fail to reach.

He readjusted the black pack on his back and shifted his bulbous green duffle bag from one hand to the other. The wind, heated to a hundred and fifteen, maybe a hundred and twenty degrees, sighed and whispered around him. Ajay's eyes swept the scrubby terrain. The endless expanse of sand, rubble and weeds in varying shades of gray, ochre, honey and rust, with here and there a gnarled tree, short as himself. The colors and textures resembled food splattered on an uneven plate that continued into oblivion. Chunks of curried potatoes in the distance. Bunches of broccoli along a dried-up gully. Chickpea boulders strewn about. Ajay's stomach growled. But he wouldn't be eating a *tagine* anytime soon, much less a tasty curry, because he didn't see even a hint of the Atlas Mountains that would signify his exit from this wretched country and entrance into Morocco. He tried not to lick his cracked lips. Though he perspired, his dark skin remained dry under the hot, blasting wind.

The wind rippled his T-shirt, one he had found in a suitcase he'd stolen two years ago. The red lettering on white cotton read *Daytona 5K Fun Run '05.*

He dropped his eyes to the scuffed black boots he'd traded for in Israel months ago and watched his feet step one after the other. Right, left, right, left, the metronome of a man walking, walking while getting ever thinner until blowing away like a paper in this unrelenting wind. And this was only May. What was this desert like in July, in August? All this because of Mother Nature, which wasn't a mother at all. Ajay felt a sudden urge to harass the elements for endangering his plans. An irrational impulse, he knew, since nature was nothing more than an automatic cycling devoid of ambition, character or soul. But Ajay turned his face heavenward and yelled anyway. "I'd rather be strangled by humidity and drowned by a monsoon flood than slowly baked like a fish!"

A gust of wind loaded with sand washed down his face and chest. Ajay coughed with his mouth closed, cheeks puffed out, the wind making a sea of his thick black hair. He shifted his green bag to his left hand and used his right to pull the worn white and red scarf from around his neck. He wiped his forehead and upper lip where a new mustache grew. There was no option other than to continue south. That or find a road leading west toward a border town where he could sell the jewelry and buy a bus ticket to the coast.

He'd walked, hitchhiked, ridden on boats and taken buses. He'd made his way to Algiers until all that remained was to get to Morocco where he could lift enough souvenir money from tourists to buy passage on a freighter bound for New York. But instead of continuing west, he'd been forced south into the desert. Ajay fingered the bulge of stolen merchandise in the right pocket of his worn trousers, the necklaces, bracelets and rings he'd stolen yesterday from a shop in Algiers. A theft the idiot police had somehow confused with a series of crimes committed by a terrorist group, forcing Ajay to hop onto the back of a vegetable truck heading out of the city. But then a police vehicle had approached from the opposite direction and signaled the truck driver to stop. If they caught him now, he'd be taken back to Algiers and interrogated in a nondescript building labeled something innocuous like *Security Forces' Center of Inquiry.* Or worse, he'd disappear forever through a doorway of a building marked only by a street number. Ajay slipped off the tailgate and hid behind a boulder, thinking he could catch a ride with the next passing vehicle. But not one had passed.

Ajay looked skyward, the expanse clear of all clouds, all moisture. The air heavy with the smell of crushed rock. After a time, he stepped off the path and walked toward a boulder. He scanned the surface for scorpions and seeing none, set his bag on the ground and jumped atop the rock. He squatted and took a green glass bottle from his pack. He swallowed two sips and licked his upper lip, then lifted the bottle to let the sun shine through. The container was less than half full. At least the wind had been at his back, pushing him forward instead of backward. For this he thanked Allah, Krishna, the Jesus god, Big Buddha and all other deities, even those he didn't know about. Then he prayed aloud to his true savior.

"God of Luck, transport me," and raising a hand to the heavens, paused, then said, "to Montana."

Montana, the land of John Wayne. Of horses and ranch life. Of the green grass he'd seen in movies and photos, the cool, snow-covered mountains in the distance. A place of opportunity, which if missed, might go to someone else.

He stared at the face of a cliff about two hundred meters across the rubbled field, the yellow bleached so pale the rock appeared almost white except for a small black scar in the middle. Ajay stretched his arm out, thumb up, and squinted. From this distance the blemish was about the size of his thumb. He lowered his arm and studied the contrast of black on white. A sheet of bone with a burn at its center. Ajay lowered his head to his hands. Another minute of rest and he'd have to move on. There were two, maybe three hours left of sunlight in which to look for water.

When he lifted his eyes again, the scar on the sheer rock face had shifted. Where before the black had been skewed like two crossed sticks, the mark now resembled a crescent moon that even as he watched bloomed into a spidery stretch of limbs creeping downward. Two arms, two legs, a head.

Ajay shot to his feet, smiling now. That was a human climbing down the cliff, a human who Ajay would somehow persuade to help him get water and food. Though why a man would climb a cliff in the middle of nowhere, Ajay didn't know. There must be a village nearby, one hidden in a hollow of land among these hills. Ajay shielded his eyes from the sun and squinted at the sight. The climber wore loose dark pants and a sleeveless top that gave full view of his thin arms. The climber's wild, shoulder-length black hair — only a little longer than Ajay's — twisted in the breeze. The climber stretched out his leg until his foot found purchase, then extended his other leg.

The climber seemed naked somehow. A person stripped to nothing but the essentials of strength and desire. He didn't even use equipment. No shoes, no belt with metal clips hanging off, not even a safety rope. As though he didn't care if he lived or died. He continued down in a slow flow. The sweeping of an arm. A leg creeping out. The head arcing from right to left. One moment the climber was a slim, curved boat and the next, a thief ready to spring into motion.

Pebbles skittered down the rock face, accompanied by tiny puffs of dust, barely visible at this distance. The climber lost his footing and his left arm flew free so that he hung by only one hand.

Ajay leaned forward. "Live, you idiot," he whispered.

But the climber didn't move to save himself. He twisted in the breeze, his hair flying about his down-turned face.

Then the climber's left foot rose and lodged on a curve of rock. He lifted his left hand and found a hold. The right leg followed. All limbs now anchored, the man remained still, a lizard in the sun. Resting.

The climber continued down and dropped the last meter or so to the ground. He took something from his mouth and crouched for a long moment. Then he rose, growing, unfolding – the movement so fluid and endless that it seemed magical. At full height, the man looked a head taller than Ajay. The climber didn't have the chest-forward posture of a man who liked to cause trouble, but that didn't mean anything. If he didn't value his own life, he wouldn't price a stranger's any higher.

The climber tilted his head toward the sky and yelled something. Ajay flew his eyes to the top of the cliff. Yet no one appeared or shouted in return. The climber picked up a small bundle from the ground and slung it on his shoulder. Then he turned and, with his eyes on the ground, began to walk swiftly across the rubble-strewn desert towards Ajay. If he'd looked up, he would have seen Ajay, but he didn't, which gave Ajay a long, clear view until the climber was only a few steps away.

And what Ajay saw through the thin cloth of the sleeveless garment as the figure approached were the erect nipples of two small breasts and a smooth mound of crotch where the light breeze blew the garment against her body. A young woman. The climber was a young woman, one who walked with an easy swing to her arms, her bare feet moving light and sure over the sand, rock and brittle weeds. She looked about his age and in her hand carried what appeared to be a wooden flute, the object she must have carried between her teeth while climbing. A flute! The odds astronomical, of meeting not just a human, but a woman, and not just a woman, but a musician like himself. While Ajay had never climbed to the top of a cliff to play for a desert — not when he could earn money from a crowd — he understood the urge. To just play.

Ajay shifted his weight. A pebble rolled off the boulder and bounced on a rock. *Ping*.

The woman, now only ten paces away, stopped, her eyes on him, their color that of the light green glass of his water bottle when the sun shone through. Unexpected decisiveness amid so much pastel. The unblinking orbs held his so tightly a long moment passed before he realized she was smiling at him.

Ajay stepped back, his right heel hanging off the edge of the boulder. An almost naked woman in a Muslim country wouldn't smile at an unknown male in public, much less when she was alone. Again he glanced right and left. No one. Yet she smiled.

He narrowed his eyes and focused on her lips. Then he realized the smile was not really a smile, but rather a false grin made by a scar, a shiny, smooth, impermeable scar. The thick rope of pink pulled down her left eye, ran a jagged semicircle around the outside of her high cheekbone and tugged up on the left corner of her mouth.

A permanent expression of sad amusement, though her eyes gave no indication of her thoughts.

The woman dropped the bundle on the ground. Ajay crouched, ready to jump backward, the boulder between them. But the woman squatted beside her bundle, from which she pulled an off-white robe. She shook it, apparently to ensure no dangerous creatures lurked in the folds, and then pulled it on over her body. She wrapped a matching scarf around her head and slipped her feet into worn sandals. Then she slung the bundle over her shoulder again, and without looking at Ajay, walked past him towards the east. He stood with unblinking eyes and an open mouth, watching this lone young woman who not only turned her back on a male stranger, but pretended he didn't exist. This crazy woman who walked in the opposite direction he wanted to go. Yet he needed water. He jumped from the boulder, slung his backpack over his shoulder and grabbed his bag.

"*Marhaba*," Ajay shouted in passable Arabic. *"Kaifa haluka?"* How are you?

Because he really did want to know.

CHAPTER 2

The climber crossed the dirt road, headed up a rise of rock and disappeared down the other side. He ran after her, his feet sliding in the sand.

"Kaifa haluka," he shouted. Then again and again. He ran with his eyes on the ground to watch for rocks and holes. Several times he glanced up to keep sight of the young woman, who was oddly far beyond him. The third time he looked up, however, he dug his heels in, leaned back and stopped. The woman stood two paces away, staring at him, her head tilted to one side. Though Ajay breathed hard, he smiled. He opened his mouth to speak, but the climber spoke first.

"Kaifa haluka is for a man," she said, her voice a trampled gravel. *"Kaifa haluki* is what you say to a female."

Ajay licked his dry lips. He nodded and smiled. He opened his mouth again, and again she spoke first.

"You'll have to negotiate with my aunt." She turned and walked away, the wind from the east making her robe flap about her ankles. The late afternoon sun made the off-white cloth a rich cream.

Ajay slung his pack on his back and jogged. He caught up and fell into step beside her.

"You don't have to worry about me acting inappropriately," he said. "I'm engaged to a woman in America. My name is Ajay. It means *sun*."

The young woman kept her eyes on her feet, her calm neither

polite nor aloof. Strands of her curly black hair brushed over her hilly lips. Her skin was the color of tea two sips from being finished. Beautiful, yet the scar…

"I didn't mean to surprise you, back there," Ajay said. He looked at the flute in the young woman's left hand. "I see you're a musician. Would you play something for me?"

The young woman walked on without replying.

"I'm a musician, too," Ajay said. He lifted the green bag. "I like to listen to other musicians. Here I find you with a flute and I think to myself, I'd like to hear her play. You carried your flute all the way up the cliff and back, so it must be important to you. You must be very good."

"I don't play for people," she said.

"You play for yourself, the true sign of an artist. If my presence bothers you, I could walk behind you. You could forget I was here."

"I don't play for people," she said again.

Ajay walked on beside the young woman, his eyes on her dark toes, callused at their tips. And how annoying, that she wouldn't play for him. Normally he could get people his own age to do as he wanted, and in particular those whom he considered to be of little regard. Such as this lone woman wandering alone in the desert. Not that he'd let her see his irritation. He jogged his shoulders and waited to talk until sure his tone would come out light and friendly."

"Perhaps yours is the best way. You don't have to play for people. But me, that's the way I earn my living; with my drums."

He halted. "Wait," he said. He swung off his pack and pulled out his bottle of water. "Do you want some water?" He took off the cap and offered her a drink. The young woman hesitated. Then she took the bottle by the neck, her fingers long and bony, the joints prominent. She lifted the opening to her nose and sniffed. She lifted the bottle, closed her eyes and drank. A drop of water escaped her mouth. The bead rounded her chin, slid down her throat and disappeared into the cloth of the headscarf.

She pulled the bottle from her lips. The container empty. Ajay stepped forward, seized the glass and turned the bottle upside down. Not a drop fell. The young woman lifted her fingertips to her lips, her eyes wide.

"I'm sorry," she whispered.

Ajay stuffed the bottle in his pack.

"Where do you live?" he said.

"In an oasis."

"Near here?"

"Not far."

"Let's go." Because she owed him now. They walked. The wind strengthened. Sand skimmed along the ground, creating a low hiss.

"Now that you drank all my water, you have to at least tell me your name," he said.

"I don't have one."

"You don't have a name?"

"No."

Ajay laughed once. The young woman walked on, her head neither lower nor higher.

"I'm not laughing at you," Ajay said. "It's just something of a coincidence, because I didn't have a name, either, when I was a child. What does your aunt call you?"

"Girl."

"Better than *boy*, I suppose."

"But my mother," the woman said, "she used to call me *Light*. 'Come here, my light.'"

"Your mother is dead?"

The woman nodded.

"And your father?"

"He is dead too."

"Your aunt doesn't let you play your flute for other people?"

"*I* don't play for people."

"But if you have a gift, why not use it?"

The young woman stopped and winged her eyes to Ajay.

"That's what my Sister Wind says," she whispered.

"What's a sister wind?"

The young woman turned and pointed toward the now distant cliff she'd climbed. "My Sister Wind lives there."

"You mean it's an actual wind?" Ajay said.

"Yes."

"What does she do, this wind?"

17

"She talks to me. She told me there's going to be a war of winds and I'm supposed to stop it. But first I have to find it."

"You have to find the war and stop it."

"Yes. That's what I'm doing, where I'm going. Back to my aunt's house for my things. Then I'll leave and go out to stop the war."

Ajay's mouth remained open for a moment, his eyes black and brilliant. "When did the wind tell you this?" he said.

"Just now. Today. Back there."

"And this war would be bad?"

"Such agony," she murmured. "It would destroy everything."

So now Ajay understood. The scar on her face was a physical symbol of her warped mind. He walked on and the young woman followed.

The sun lowered in the whitening sky. They had an hour of light, maybe less. Ajay asked what he would find in the oasis. The woman answered with a minimum of words. The village had a central well, a small store and about twenty households that totaled a hundred date farmers, camel owners and goat herders. In terms of transportation, a bus rumbled through once a week, the next one arriving five days from today. Besides the bus, a village man rented camels to tourists.

The young woman also said the village had an outpost of the rural police.

"Police," Ajay said.

"Yes. Or really only one. His name is Awad. He claims to be a relation of the once famous singer Ali Al-Khencheli, but nobody believes him."

Ajay remained silent, rock grinding beneath his boots, his mouth a trim line. A tiny village with a policeman. A bus five days from departure. A camel. Yet the village had water and food. And a policeman. And a bus that wouldn't leave for another five days. And a camel upon which anyone would look conspicuous, especially a stranger. He looked sideways at the young woman.

"Why would the winds want to war with each other?" Ajay asked.

"They don't," the woman said. "It's just— Some of the winds want to kill people for being so…"

"Rotten?"

"Thoughtless. They abuse things. They abuse the winds, they abuse the earth, they abuse—"

"Each other."

The wind had grown stronger, making the edges of the woman's headscarf flap more vigorously. "They make the earth sick and if the earth dies, the winds die," she said.

"So that's what the winds are fighting about? Some want to murder mankind and others don't?"

She nodded.

"Which side are you on?" he said.

Again the woman didn't answer. Didn't jump to mankind's rescue as most people would. Which was interesting. She wanted to save this sister wind, yet to do so, she would have to save mankind, a task she didn't seem thrilled to perform. Quite a bind.

Ajay coughed from the dust blowing down his throat. He drew his scarf from his pocket and looped the handle of his bag over his arm to free his hands. Then he tied the cloth loosely around his throat.

"When is this war supposed to happen?" Ajay said.

"I don't know," she said.

"How are you going to find it?" He pulled the scarf over his nose to test the fit.

"My Sister Wind will help me," the woman said. "And other winds."

Ajay let the scarf hang around his neck, ready for use if the wind became a problem.

They trudged up a rise of rock. At the top, wind gusted into their faces. Ajay pulled the scarf up over his nose and hoisted his green bag over his shoulder, his body a buffer against the flying dust. He leaned into the current of sand skimming the earth at knee level. He glanced at the young woman and saw that she, too, leaned forward. She held a corner of her scarf over her nose and mouth. The flying sand stung Ajay's bare forehead.

"*Bakvas*," he cursed, his throat coated in dust.

Still the wind increased, first to a shriek, then to dust so thick the horizon vanished. He felt a hand on his forearm, the woman pulling him forward through the swirling grit. She sank to her knees and turned, the wind at her back. She drew her hands and feet under her robe and tucked her head to her knees. Ajay followed her example, but instead of drawing his arms into his T-shirt, he put his green bag between his legs and hunched his upper body around the bulk. He held tight.

The sand became thousands of flying needles. Became a throat choke. Became pins in the eyes. The wind ate at the ground where Ajay sat, then built his seat back up, hundreds of fingers wiggling and digging beneath him. His hands turned to dried paper, his throat to a hot road, his eyelids to thin crusts of rock. He cursed the wind. That something as simple as moving air could dry out his instrument. His instrument, without which he would be nothing. Would have no future in America, no life, no heart.

He cocked an ear and waited. He heard the sound again, a distant shout. He opened one eye to a slit and peered through a heavy grill of eyelashes to see the young woman standing, her legs braced wide and back straight. She clutched her flute in her right hand. The wind tore at her clothes, making the curve of her body — the definition of her breasts, her hipbone — so sharp she once again seemed naked. She held her head high, her chin an immoveable cliff.

The wind shoved her sideways. She fell to her knees. She struggled to her feet, the muscles in her neck straining. She straightened and squared her shoulders against the onslaught. Her mouth opened and she screamed something unintelligible into the wind. The wind knocked her over again, and again she rose. Until at last she dropped into a ball and remained still.

Ajay closed his tearing eyes, yet the image remained, of a young woman clutching a flute, screaming into the wind. His thoughts were so intense that at first he didn't notice anything other than an easing. Soon the sand was no longer stinging his back so sharply. The wind continued to drop until finally Ajay could pull his scarf from his face. He blinked. Sand fell from his eyelashes. The wind still scurried low along the ground, but the dust in the air had thinned. The sky had turned a deep blue in the east, the sun just above the horizon in the west. The wind died to a breeze.

Ajay looked down. At where his instrument should be. He jumped to his feet and spun around. Where before he and the woman had been sitting on a low hill of sand with a view of the distant landscape, they were now in a small bowl that blocked all recognizable features. Ajay staggered around in a full circle. His eyes fell on the woman. She watched him, her face caked in dust. She pointed at his feet. Ajay fell to his knees and dug. Within moments he uncovered the green bag.

"*Bakvas*," he said. "*Dhat tereki!*"

He sat, crossed his legs and brushed the remaining sand from the bag, blowing upon it to clear the last clinging grains away. He unzipped the canvas and pulled out the two cushioned rings covered in green, orange and white-flowered fabric. He stood and walked downwind to shake the rings against his leg while cursing the dust that fell. He set the rings on the ground by the bag and made sure they were level with one another. Then he pulled out a round, silver-based drum from the bag. He brushed the goatskin top and lifted the drum to scrutinize the surface for cracks. He didn't find any. He turned the drum over and when satisfied, set the drum on the ring by his left knee. He adjusted the position so the palm-sized black circle on the drum's surface tilted away from him.

Ajay pulled a second, smaller drum from the green bag. He ran his fingertips along the carved, deep red wood. The lacings still taut, the wooden tuning pegs in place. He lowered the drum to rest on the right ring. He cocked an ear and with a finger, tapped the black eye of the right drum, then that of the left. He played a fast rhythm, letting his hands fly from one drum to the other.

After awhile he stopped, a palm resting on each drum. He nodded, though his lips remained pressed tight.

"Well it looks like your precious wind didn't kill my drums after all," he said.

"They're very important to you," the woman said.

Ajay didn't look at her. He stood and put the drums back in the bag along with the rings.

"Did you know I'm going to perform the *tabla* when I get to America?" he said. To her. To the wind. To the world. "On many stages, for huge crowds. Thousands of people. And I'm going to teach, too."

He'd get married and buy a ranch and if he wanted to, learn how to ride a horse and swim in a pool. He'd play his drums to the mountains. Ajay zipped the drum bag. He grabbed his backpack and shook it. Savagely.

"Do you realize that if I were to lose my instrument I —" But Ajay had to stop. He didn't know what he would do if he lost his drums, because he couldn't live without them and without what resided within them. He could, but he couldn't. Not really.

"What did you yell into the wind just now?" he asked.

"It was just a *Chichili*," she said. "A spring wind storm."

"I didn't ask what kind of wind it was. I asked what you yelled."

When the young woman didn't respond, Ajay said, "You told it to stop, didn't you?"

The young woman remained silent. Ajay didn't press her for an answer as he busied himself strapping his pack to his shoulders. She'd yelled and the storm had stopped. Though if she could really communicate with the wind, why not convince the storm wind to stop before it began?

"When are you planning to leave?" he said. "To find this war of winds?"

"Tonight."

"Which way are you going?"

The woman lifted her face to the sky and closed her eyes. She inhaled the air like someone drawing in the scent of an appetizing meal. She opened her eyes, turned and pointed. West.

Ajay smiled. A grim smile, but a smile nonetheless. She'd given him direction in the storm. She'd give him water from her oasis. She'd lead him back in the right direction. Then she could do what she liked with mankind. The young woman stood, turned and walked towards her village. Again Ajay followed, though this time into the descending darkness.

CHAPTER 3

The oasis appeared as a distant glimmer of stars set among the dunes. Ajay and the woman drew nearer until the illumination formed into the window glow of a dozen squat, flat-topped buildings set in chaotic order on either side of a dirt road. Just south of the oasis, the fronds of a date palm grove tossed in the evening breeze. The sun had set, leaving a wash of red on sand and buildings alike.

Ajay tapped a disjointed rhythm on his thigh with one hand. He'd instructed the woman to take him to her home. He'd told her that he would stand outside while she filled his water bottles and brought food. Then they would leave again and spend the night in the desert. When she got him to a border town, they would part and he would be on his way, though he didn't tell her this. His urgency greater now. To get away. To escape. Although he'd never encountered a circumstance from which he couldn't extract himself, this might be his last chance do so, his final opportunity to capitalize on his good luck.

An old man in a skullcap and robe led a camel down the street. A woman veiled in black pulled a bucket of water from the village's central well while a child sat in the dirt, throwing stones and laughing. Ajay licked his cracked lips and followed the young woman to a blue-curtained window at the back of a small house. She turned and put out her hand, palm up. Ajay shrugged off his pack and pulled out his green bottle. She took it and turned away from him.

"Wait," he said and dug out two larger empty plastic bottles. The young woman set the bottles on one side of the window ledge and jumped up to sit on the other. She swung her legs over the windowsill and disappeared behind the curtain, which seemed to breathe in and out in the evening breeze.

Ajay walked a few steps towards the corner of the home and peered out. Across the dirt road was the small store/café the young woman had mentioned. A dog of short-bristled fur and visible ribs trotted down the street. Just past the well was a white Land Rover with an official emblem painted on the side door. The vehicle was parked in front of a gray building. The policeman's desert palace.

Ajay heard a small noise behind him. He turned. The young woman leaned out the window. She held the green bottle, now full and dripping water, along with the other two plastic containers. He squatted and put them in his backpack. Again he heard the small noise. This time she held a yellow plastic bucket half full of water. He set the bucket on the sand and with both hands scooped up mouthful after mouthful until his stomach was full. Then he splashed a little on his face and arms, soaked his scarf and drank the last. He handed the bucket back to the young woman.

"And food?" he whispered.

The young woman nodded.

"Girl?" a voice called from within the house.

Though the woman's eyes remained on Ajay, they lost all expression. She didn't move.

"Girl?" The voice moved closer, the pitch sharper.

"How much longer do you need?" he whispered.

"Not much," the young woman said.

Ajay turned and walked quickly around the back corner of the house and towards the front corner. He glanced both ways along the dirt road, now deserted, then hustled to the front door. He knocked on the wood, his mind rifling through excuses for why he'd come. Then he noticed an old wooden table to the left of the door. Atop the table was a basket containing dates and another holding three blood oranges.

An old woman leaned out a window next to the front door. Dressed in black. The face of a pitted rock with two black eyes. She clasped her hands, the thin, veined fingers adorned with silver rings. An ugly woman who apparently adored wearing pretty things.

The aunt's mouth curved into a smile.

"I'd like to buy some fruit," Ajay said.

The aunt looked him over. Her smile deepened. Her eyes paused on his drum bag, then moved to his face. "A tourist?" she said in a high voice that climbed higher with the question.

"Yes."

Her eyes glanced up and down the street, then back to him. "How did you get here?"

"I walked."

Her eyebrows lifted, then her eyes narrowed. That a foreigner would walk out of the desert at night.

"Did you get caught in the wind storm?" she said.

"Yes."

"The wind is strange this time of year. It starts. It stops." The old woman shrugged. "You are lucky it stopped. It could easily have buried you." Again she smiled. "What would you like?" She spread a hand toward the table. The fruit dry and bruised. The remains of what other people hadn't bought that day.

"The price is cheap, for you," the old woman said. "It is the end of the day and there will be no more customers tonight."

"How much?" Ajay said.

"Six hundred *dinar*."

Six hundred dinar. Over three hundred rupees. Almost eight American dollars. For a few dates and oranges.

Ajay smiled. One thief to another. "That's a ridiculous price for old fruit spoiled by the heat of the day," he said.

The old woman feigned surprise. "It is what I normally charge my customers." She lowered her voice to a confidential tone. "Though this fruit may be wilted, the fruit I keep inside is always moist and young. Very tasty." The aunt tilted her head back, not to the fruit, but towards the interior of the house. Towards merchandise within. "Because you look particularly famished, I'll only charge you five hundred *dinar*."

You'll have to negotiate with my aunt.

Old Aunt smiled.

Ajay considered Old Aunt. The reason, maybe, the young

woman was crazy.

Ajay shook his head. "I'm not that hungry."

"Come now," the old aunt said, her small eyes closing halfway. "You look emaciated. What you need is nourishment for that—" and her glance lingered on his private parts, "that young, aching body of yours."

A door across the road behind Ajay opened and banged shut. The door of the police station. Old Aunt's gaze flowed over Ajay's shoulder to whoever had come out of the door. Her face melted to liquid sugar.

"Marhaba," the aunt said.

Ajay wiped his nose with the back of his hand and in the process nipped a glance behind him. The uniformed policeman ignored Old Aunt. A man of thick upper body, he strode next door to the café like he was in a hurry - this man who was probably too stupid to hold a higher position in a more important place, yet ambitious enough to crave notoriety through the capture of a terrorist.

The policeman yanked the store's front door and entered. Light the color of golden oil poured out along with the smell of lamb and cinnamon. He wouldn't be in there for long, not a busy man like that.

A camel bellowed. Ajay flattened his damp scarf on the table. He placed the fruit in the center of the square, tied up the ends and put the bundle in his backpack. When he looked up, Old Aunt was no longer smiling. Voices sounded behind him. Of the policeman and another male. The policeman laughed.

Normally Ajay would bargain with the woman and pay her as little as possible. But tonight he drew a thin gold bangle from his pocket and laid the gold on the wooden table. An item followed by Old Aunt's unblinking eyes. She disappeared from the window, reappeared in the doorway and glided toward the jewelry.

The door of the store/café creaked open. The policeman laughed again. Ajay sauntered around the corner of the house, then moved quickly to the young woman's window and brushed the curtains aside. The room was empty. He hadn't been more than a few minutes.

"Girl!" Aunt yelled.

Ajay ran towards the open desert in the direction from which he — they — had come. He struggled up a sand rise and dropped down the other side. He scanned the rock, sand and hills. Though the full moon illuminated the desert, nothing moved. He'd bought time for her escape and she returned the deed by escaping him. He cursed her long legs and ran. The pack thumped his back while the green bag banged against his leg. The wind pushed from behind. But even so, he had to stop and bend over to catch his breath. The first star pricked the blackness. The burning day now slid fast toward a seventy-degree night, the cool wind making Ajay shiver.

Maybe she never left the oasis. Maybe she liked being a whore. Some women did. Yet that possibility did not seem to match a woman who yelled at a storm a million times more powerful than a single human.

Ajay squinted into the distance. There. Then again. He leaned forward, but the movement disappeared, or had never occurred. But then there appeared a ripple and sway amid the stillness. He ran. He slipped and fell to his knees and rose to run again, the water in his belly sloshing. Sweat fell from his temples. He kept on towards the movement that developed into a river of cloth waving in the moonlight until the undulation became a single figure walking into a harsh, dead world. A fellow mover and reveler in things unsaid. Go. Do. Be. The near panic Ajay had felt when he thought he had lost the woman now turned to a feeling of relief. And something else. A feeling sharp and irreversible – a deep cut on its way to a scar – that though painful, felt strangely pleasant. He would help this woman, one forced to whore for her keep, making her, like him, a person without a home. He would help her and she would be grateful.

When he got close enough, he yelled at her to stop. But she didn't. He gained on her and yelled again. When he got within five strides, the young woman whipped around. Her eyes glowed in the moonlight, white gems. She held a kitchen knife thin of blade, worn of handle and sharp at the tip. He didn't move, and neither did she.

"Don't try to stop me," she said.

"All right."

"At any point."

"Right."

She not wanting him to stop her. He not wanting her to stop him. How a purpose could burn in one's chest, making a person of no

27

means go farther than he, or she, ever thought possible.

The young woman lowered her arm. She slid her knife into her bundle, but kept her intensity on Ajay.

"I have to warn you, though," she said. "Traveling with me might be dangerous."

Ajay didn't laugh. Although it was so funny, to say he could be in danger only moments after she'd threatened him with a knife.

"Why?" he said.

"The winds who want to kill humans, they're going to try and stop me. And anyone who goes with me."

Ajay glanced behind him. Toward the oasis and Old Aunt, who would soon find her merchandise gone and no doubt want to report the theft.

"How many days will it take to get to Morocco?" Ajay said.

The young woman again cocked her head as if to listen. Ajay listened, too, but all he heard was the low moan of a wind that rose and ebbed.

"Three days," the woman said.

"And we have enough food and water?"

"I think so."

"Do you have identity papers?" Ajay said.

"Yes."

"A passport?"

"A passport?"

"Yes."

"No."

Ajay moved his tongue around his teeth. If she didn't have a passport, she probably didn't have a travel visa, which meant they were in the same predicament. Crossing the border without the documents would be risky and expensive. But maybe one of her winds could fly Ajay and her to where they needed to go.

"Let's make a deal, you and I," Ajay said. "You get me to the border town and then you can go your way and I'll go mine. That way you don't have to worry about me trying to stop you and I don't have to worry about one of your winds killing me. Yes?"

"They're not *my* winds," she said. "And you're supposed to come with me."

"What?"

28

CHAPTER 4

The young woman tilted her head upward briefly, then turned her eyes towards Ajay.

"My Sister Wind sent you to help me find where it will happen, this war," she said.

"Sent me to help you?" Ajay said.

"Yes."

Her Sister Wind told her to expect an assistant and Ajay had appeared. Or maybe her Sister Wind hadn't given any specific instructions, but simply said, *Go forth and stop the war, and by the way, good luck doing the job alone.* The gargantuan chore, the impossible task. So that when Ajay happened by, the young woman worked him into her fantasy, a recruit to share the headache of saving the world.

Ajay glanced behind him. Expecting the headlights of the policeman's white Land Rover. He walked faster, but the woman maintained her pace. He angled to the right, toward a ridge of rock behind which maybe they could walk undetected, but she kept to her course. Ajay angled back to her. There had to be a strategy for getting a crazy woman to move faster and with more care. Then he snapped his fingers.

"If we're going to travel together for awhile, I'll need to know what to call you," he said. The woman followed him down a dune where they stopped below a rock ledge. Now out of sight of anyone coming from the east, he could give her something. The best kind of something, too, which was something that cost nothing. He squatted and opened his backpack. He pulled out and donned a frayed maroon sweater then fished out a thin, hand-sized paperback with a light blue cover featuring cartoon storks carrying diapered babies through the sky. The young woman squatted beside him and watched him open the only book he carried. Though crazy, she made a wonderful audience with the intensity of her gaze. Ajay scanned the pages, but the brightness of the moon could not quite light the words. He dug in his backpack again and pulled out a small flashlight.

"As I told you, I had no name, either," he said. "My mother or father left me in an alley and an old woman found me." Though after so many years, the old woman was more a feel — of a hand resting on his head — than the memory of a face or action.

"She died when I was four or five, so I don't remember what she called me. Maybe *boy*." Ajay smiled. The young woman looked at him. Then the right corner of her mouth lifted. Ajay smiled deeper. That a person could be crazy and yet have a sense of humor.

"So when I got old enough, I decided to pick a name for myself," Ajay said. "But by that time I'd learned it was depressing to lose what you got attached to. So I didn't allow myself to get attached to anything, including names. I told myself that whenever I needed to — or wanted to — I'd change my name. That's why I carry this book around."

"What's the book about?" she said.

"It's not about anything," Ajay said. "It's just a list of names."

"I don't understand."

Ajay opened the book and turned the flashlight on the page. He ran his finger down a column and stopped at a name. He turned the book halfway towards the young woman and read the name he pointed to.

"Mahibala," he said. "Do you like it? It means *sweet girl*."

But when the young woman rolled her lips together and frowned, Ajay consulted the page again.

"Or you could be a goddess," he said. "Why not, yes? Mahadevi, the Goddess Parvati. Very grand. Or Mahalakshmi. That's Goddess Lakshmi."

The young woman dropped her eyes to the ground and stroked an eyebrow. At the pressure, perhaps, of choosing a name when she'd never had one. Or maybe she thought Ajay was making fun of her, suggesting a desert whore who had nothing but a flute should call herself a goddess. Ajay moved his eyes slower down the list. He pointed to a name.

"I think you should be Madina," Ajay said.

"Why should I be a c*ity*, a *town?*

"What?" Ajay read the definition of the name again. "It says here it means *land of beauty.*"

"*Medina* does not mean land of beauty."

Ajay read the text. "But it says here *dark...*" Then again, *medina* does mean *city*, in Arabic. He could explain the difference in spelling, but she seemed to like stories more than reality. He thought a moment, his eyes on the stars. "Where I come from, it means *land of beauty*. Since my name means sun, it seems right you should be *land of beauty*," and Ajay gestured to the desert he hoped to leave and never see again, "because that's where the sun shines."

The young woman lifted her face to the sky. What she did, apparently, when she wanted to ask the opinion of her wind friends.

The young woman looked at Ajay and smiled. He blew out a breath and would have smiled had he not been annoyed by how difficult she'd been to persuade for a woman who'd never had a name before. By the time he stuffed the book into his backpack, the young woman had already walked away, her pace faster now. More determined. No one would be able to stop this woman convinced she had to save the world, much less a policeman who claimed to be a relation of the once famous singer Ali Al-Khencheli.

When Ajay caught up to the woman, he said, "Now Madina. How is it you can talk to the wind?"

CHAPTER 5

Ajay and Madina walked deep into the cool night. Despite his exhaustion, there was satisfaction in knowing each step taken was one farther from the police and one less to endure under a homeless sky. The time passed. The wind blew. The moon crossed the sky and Madina told her tale of winds, a world so rich Ajay's mind folded around the telling. As she talked, he studied the shadowed contours of contrasting darkness and imagined the land a burial ground of kings, once fabulous kings, but now dead.

Madina said that a long time ago, the desert was not a desert, but a land of boundless beauty. There were blue lakes and silver rivers through expanses of tall grass and forest. Animals wandered in harmony with people because there was enough food for everyone. The sun shone, the rains came, the winds blew without rancor. Paradise, nirvana, heaven, a state of delight, a deliverance from ignorance and disharmony. Not something a person of intelligence could believe, but who could argue against the temptation of the idea?

In Madina's past paradise, people could talk to the winds, which could share their wisdom, pass on warnings and even gossip. If a man got lost while out hunting, all he had to do was cup a hand to his mouth and yell the name of the place where he lived. The wind would roll the sound off a distant mountain and the returning echo would tell him which way to go. If crops needed water, farmers could ask the winds to push rain clouds over the planted fields.

The next part of the story proved predictable. Over time, humans decided they were superior to the land and other animals and grew distant from both. People took more food and water than they needed or deserved. And when the land flooded or the earth quaked, when the wind blew too hard or lightning struck, people cursed the earth and the wind alike.

The winds reminded people these events were part of the world, part of life, and that if people accepted the laws of nature, they wouldn't be so afraid and disappointed. But humans wouldn't listen. In their selfishness, they turned away from the winds. After awhile, most of the winds stopped speaking to people. Most, but not all.

Time went on and the human race grew. The more people there were, the more they needed. They drained the lakes to appease their thirst and that of their crops. They enslaved other animals or killed them for fun. Humans sent filth into the air from inventions they created and from forests they burned. The filth made the winds sluggish, sick and angry enough to push rain clouds away from the planted fields. The crops withered and died. Years of drought set in. Lakes dried up. Water and food dwindled. People drifted away, abandoning one village after another. The winds ground down once great cities into dust and swept the remains away. The winds were sorry to see the other animals disappear and the grasses and trees die. Yet however much the winds hated the destruction, they hated people even more.

Now the winds roamed this land freely. They sculpted the rock and sand into ever-changing shapes. Most of the desert winds retained the bitterness man brought to earth. But there were those who mourned the lost happiness and peace so deeply they continued to search for people who would listen and help create paradise once again.

A pebble shifted underfoot. Ajay hopped sideways to avoid a twisted ankle. He shook his head at his lapse in vigilance, then turned in a full circle, to check for approaching headlights. But there were none. He fingered his mustache and considered Madina's story.

"Do you talk to winds like we talk?" Ajay said. "Out loud? With words?"

"We don't need words."

"What do you do, then, talk to one another in your head?"

Madina tilted her face to the sky, apparently unable to provide an answer without first seeking a consultation.

"It's not really thinking so much as feeling," Madina said. "Knowing the currents and how they curve and where they prod. Where they hide. How they burst forth. The wash of it all around you."

The wind blew through the holes in Ajay's sweater. He shivered.

"How many other people can talk to the wind?" he said.

"None," Madina said.

"You're the only person in the entire world who can talk to the winds?"

"That's what my Sister Wind says."

"Having to save mankind must be a terrible burden," Ajay said.

Madina shrugged, as though saving the world was just something one had to do. Ajay was silent for a moment, reflecting on this strange lunacy. Caused, he decided, because some people couldn't take the rigors of life. The weaker dragged into alleys by the stronger. The starving robbed of their last morsel of food. Those who collapsed under the rules of survival didn't understand the moment of abuse was just an unlucky point in time, nothing more. Instead they allowed the unpleasantness to take root and grow into a monstrosity they had no choice but to carry, but somehow managed to ignore. Blindness so tempting, so indulgent. Better they be made stronger. Made to see.

"What was it like, living with your aunt?" Ajay said.

Madina remained silent.

"Did she make you work hard?" He waited, but she didn't reply. "A woman like that seems like she would make you work for your keep. Did you cook and clean? Did you take in laundry? What kind of chores did she make you do?"

Madina shook her head. "It doesn't matter—"

"It does matter," Ajay said. "What a person does with her life matters."

Madina shook her head. "The wind—"

"But I'm not talking about the wind. I'm talking about you."

35

Madina stopped, her eyes on the ground. She didn't stroke her eyebrow. She didn't tighten her lips.

Her expression melted from rigid to calm. She lifted her eyes to the sky, her face to the breeze.

"It was so empty here, when I first came," she said. "I was from a city down south and there were more people. And here— nobody. If there had been anybody, a lot of rushing around and noise— But here there was nothing. Nothing to do but listen." The right side of her mouth lifted. "When I listened, I heard." She looked at Ajay. Looked into him, who he was, and without anger.

"My winds," she said. "They'll never leave me."

Implying he would.

Madina reared out of sleep, body rocketing forward to a sitting position and arms flying wide. She remained that way, breathing hard, the moon casting her shadow. She lowered her shaking arms. She licked her lips and drew the back of her hand across her sweating forehead. She glanced to the left, where Ajay lay a few meters away, curled into himself, his back to her.

Madina rose and in the bright night, stepped away to a place behind a boulder and squatted to relieve herself.

By the time she returned, Ajay had shifted to his back, arms flung outward, as hers had been when she awoke, the fingers curling upward. She smiled a little. Instead of returning to her spot, she stepped closer to him, until her toes almost touched his side. Her eyes moved from his splayed feet, up his legs, past his concave belly to his chest. Though the maroon sweater was dark, the moon provided enough light to see a tiny shadow on his rib cage, more towards his heart than not.

Madina held her breath for a moment. Then she parted her lips. Air slipped in and out without a sound. She slowly lowered to her haunches and rested her hands atop her knees. A strand of hair caught on her eyelash, but she didn't move to push it away. She stared at what made the shadow; at the curled tail and the pincers lifted and ready. The scorpion didn't move.

Madina slid her eyes left, letting them range as far as possible, then to the right, where they stopped on a thin camel bush twig. She shifted her body to the right while reaching out an arm until her thumb and forefinger closed on the brittle, bleached twig. She shifted back to center until her weight was fully on both feet. Then she tilted her ear toward the sky. She seemed to listen, then nodded. She righted her head and waited, the stick poised above Ajay like a conductor.

The scorpion scrambled towards Ajay's throat. Madina's arm snapped out. The creature disappeared. She shot to her feet, strode around Ajay, and spying where the scorpion had landed, smashed the arachnid with her sandal-shod foot.

She stroked her eyebrow and swallowed. She dropped the stick and turned to Ajay, who hadn't moved. She walked around him and lay down, though closer this time. She fell asleep.

CHAPTER 6

Ajay had never thought he could grow irritated by blue sky. But he had never before experienced a prolonged period under blue skies in the desert. After catching a few hours of sleep, he and Madina again trudged beneath an expanse brutal in its clarity. Maybe if they prayed to the God of Luck they'd find shade before the sand and rock began radiating heat. At least they'd reach the border town tomorrow, an eventuality that though close in time felt distant due to the sameness of a broken landscape that gave one the feeling of walking in place. Boring, maddening, never-ending.

"Who had green eyes?" Ajay said. "In your family, I mean."

Madina shrugged. "I don't know much about my family."

"Your aunt. Didn't she tell you anything about your relatives?"

"She never talked to me much."

"What about your mother?"

"What about your family?" Madina said, her tone a veil across her being.

"I told you I was an orphan," Ajay said.

"What did you do when the old woman died?"

Ajay jogged ahead, turned and walked backward in front of Madina. "Well, at first I sat down and cried. Then a scrawny cat came along. But I didn't have anything to feed it so it lost interest and wandered away." What he didn't tell her was how the cat stopped, turned its head and stared at him with eyes the same color as Madina's. "And I thought, 'Well maybe the cat knows what to do.'

So I followed."

"And did he?"

"It showed me everything. Where to hide, where to sleep, where to find food, how to escape without a sound. Mostly, though, the cat taught me the world is plentiful and I should take what I wanted whenever I wanted it."

Ajay turned forward and fell into place beside Madina.

"What happened to the cat?" she said.

Ajay touched a finger to his mustache. "It got trampled by a cow. So I cooked it and ate it, or what was left of it, anyway."

A long moment passed.

"You must have been very hungry," she said.

Ajay didn't look at her. After a long moment, he nodded.

That night Ajay sat on a boulder near the campfire and pushed a lump of couscous into his mouth. A few particles fell onto his chin. He brushed the grains off into a cupped hand and licked his palm clean. Rice was better. Larger and less likely to fall out of one's mouth. He inhaled, almost smelling rice and a curry, maybe some *dhal* and a warm *naan*. He licked his lips. Tomorrow he'd buy a real meal when he and Madina reached Morocco.

Madina sat with her knees pulled tight to her chin near the fire made from dead brushwood they'd found along a dried-up gully. A *wadi*, Madina had said. Whispery clouds sailed past a full moon, the landscape a shadowed bright. Now that Madina had told him her story about the winds, he could see, in the dried-up riverbeds, the broad valleys reduced to rubble, the air sharp with emptiness, the land that used to exist.

Ajay felt uneasy, though he didn't know why. He and Madina had enough water, fruit and goat cheese for one more meal. They hadn't seen anyone, yet he felt more exposed, like they were being watched. And not by a policeman, either, but by someone who knew something bad was going to happen and wanted to be there to see the show. The feeling would either become real — something he could deal with — or evaporate.

Madina and all her talk of destruction. A form of doom he'd only have to endure for one more day, though. Which meant he only had twenty-four hours in which to learn how Madina got her scar.

Sand skimmed the barren hills. A low hissing that lifted and died away.

"What's it saying now, the wind?" Ajay said.

Madina cocked an ear. "Sometimes winds don't say anything, they just pass."

"You know," Ajay said, "there are people who specialize in predicting weather. They talk about barometers and air pressure and precipitation. To them wind is just a scientific phenomenon. Something that blows hot or cold, carries seeds, moves clouds around." He shrugged. "What other purpose does it have?"

"Each wind has its own job," Madina said. "To push or pull. To pull in or suck out. If there's too much movement, the winds seep away. If there's too little, they rush in. Always wanting…"

"Wanting what?"

"Balance."

"Peace."

Madina seemed to consider the word. "Yes. Peace."

The fire popped and crackled, the red sinking into a liquid ripple of white coals. Madina spread her hand out to encompass the desert. "If every grain of sand in this desert represented one thing to know about the wind—" and she scooped up a handful of sand, "—this is how much of it people understand." She tilted her palm and let the sand leak out until none remained.

"But they've got proof certain winds do certain things, go particular places," Ajay said. "The winds must obey some kind of rules even if they are spirits, or whatever it is you say they are. Within some boundaries—"

"Yes, but—"

"Like your sister wind. Why do you have to go to the cliff to see her when it would be simpler and faster if she traveled to you, yes?"

"She rides high along the cliffs," Madina said. "If she travels lower or far from her region, she could blend with another wind and lose herself."

Ajay slid off his boulder and sat cross-legged beside her.

41

"Don't all winds blend?"

"At their edges, but their centers remain intact."

"Like married people." Ajay laughed.

"Some winds—" Madina said. She stroked an eyebrow. On the brink. She had been waiting — for how long? — to tell someone about what she loved best. Wanting to share, yet wanting to protect, too. She pressed her lips tight, but they opened, anyway.

"Some winds flow constantly in one direction because of the way the earth turns," she said. Once begun, she couldn't stop. She draped her winds for him to view. The Worker Winds that pushed storm clouds and Guard Winds that kept people off sacred mountains. Powerful winds that crossed oceans, bringing news to land-bound winds. Some winds came at certain times of the day, or only during certain seasons, like the *Chichili*, which swept the desert clean.

Though Madina kept her voice low and well-paced, her tone vibrated with an energy that increased until almost seething from the intensity of her outpouring. About how the size of a wind determined the distance a current could travel. Her Sister Wind, for example, was a regional wind and could move only so far from her normal boundaries. Smaller winds had to remain local to a village, or even a house, unless they caught a ride on a larger wind. Though they didn't have much power and died easily, they were the most flexible. They slipped in and out of tight places and often enjoyed wrapping themselves around people, which was why Madina called them Land Lovers. In contrast, some winds were loners and never came close to land. One in particular apparently circled high above the earth and kept an eye on other winds.

"Couldn't a wind like that watch out for evil winds?" Ajay said. "Maybe look down and if it saw the bad winds having a meeting, rush down and break it up? That would stop the war so you wouldn't have to, yes?"

"No."

"Why not?"

Madina made her hands into fists and placed them over her mouth. After a moment she lowered her hands. "I can't tell you."

Ajay leaned forward. "You can't because you don't know, or because you know, but can't tell me?"

42

Madina said nothing.

"A secret," Ajay murmured. Knowing there is a way into every locked house and into every secret.

"What about these evil winds, the ones that want to kill me?" Ajay said.

"They're not evil."

"If they want to kill me, they're evil."

Madina brushed the sand off her toes. "They're not evil."

"Fine. The anti-human winds. What are they called and where do they come from?"

"I don't know much about them," Madina said. "My Sister Wind says I'll know them when I feel them."

A lick of wind rolled around Ajay's neck. Invisible fingers slipping down his shirt. He jerked and the tingle vanished.

"I think you're wrong about there not being evil winds," Ajay said. "Just like in war. There's always an evil element. An instigator. The clever one who stirs up trouble by whispering well-placed lies here and there and then steps back to watch the stupid soldiers fight." Ajay stroked his mustache. "And anyway, what would this war of winds do to the earth?"

Madina stared into the fire for a long time. Then she lay down and turned her back to him. Story time apparently over. Ajay tilted his face up. He listened to the crackle of the fire and the lowing of the wind. Wondering what it would be like to be murdered — everyone murdered — by winds gone wild?

The sound came into his sleep as a soughing of wind. The lift and fall a murmurous sadness. A rise that began to choke, pulling Ajay up until his eyes fluttered open. To the infinite stars, and that sound.

He lay on his left side, his knees tucked up and blanket half over his head against the cold, undulating wind, and beneath that, the *mm mm mm*, so strangled. A sound that came from behind. He rolled to his back and looked sideways to where Madina lay on her back. Arms at her sides. Fingers twitching. Lips struggling to open. And though her eyes were closed, she frowned, her jaw muscles tight. *Mm mm mm*.

Ajay reached out. He patted her forehead with his fingertips.

43

Her brow loosened. The muscles of her face relaxed. The soughing lessened and stopped, her lips still and slightly open. The contours of profile blending with the hills and dips in the distance.

Ajay pulled his arm back. He watched her a moment longer, then rolled back to his side. And slept.

The next day at midday, Madina stopped by a tope-colored boulder the size of a two-story house, yet casting only a half-body sliver of shade. She cocked an ear and squinted into a noon sky almost white from the dust hanging in the air. No animals scuttled. No wind blew. The heat pressed down, its weight staggering.

Ajay rubbed his dry eyes. "The town we're heading for is near the mountains, yes? Mountains are big. People have told me you can see them from far, far away. Not something easily missed, in other words. Well, I don't see any mountains."

Madina slipped off her shoes and put her calloused hands on the hot rock.

Ajay grabbed the back of her robe and pulled her off. "You can't climb dressed like that. You'll fall."

Madina turned around to face him. Tall. Her gaze still and silent. "Don't do that."

"Then don't be an idiot."

He set down his drum bag, took off his backpack and pulled his shirt over his head. He handed it to her. She averted her eyes from his bare chest. Ajay smiled. But she didn't. Not at all. A modest whore, then, refusing to be reminded of her recently-escaped servitude.

Madina accepted his shirt and changed behind the boulder. She emerged with her eyes down and arms at her side, the cloth stretched tight across her shoulders and stopping just above the waist of her loose white pants, revealing a sliver of dark abdomen. Her discomfort proof she could be gotten to and ruffled despite the massive fortification of her inner *casbah*.

"Are we lost?" he said.

She turned and leapt at the boulder, soon out of sight beyond the curve leading to the top.

Ajay sat in the dwindling shade of the boulder. His skin dry and marbled white by powdery rivulets of salt residue from perspiration that evaporated before appearing.

"Are we lost?" he yelled up at her.

But she didn't answer. Too busy trying to find a wind from which to get directions. They still had a plastic bottle of water, a handful of dates, one orange and some goat cheese of wicked odor.

He opened his drum bag and set the drums before him, all the while shaking his head. That he could be so stupid as to assume that because she lived in the desert she would know how to navigate one, when in all probability, she never left the oasis other than to climb her cliff and return home.

Ajay played a slow rhythm on his drums.

"I've heard of people who got stranded in the desert and had to drink radiator fluid from their cars, and even blood," Ajay yelled.

Madina hopped down from the boulder, retrieved her robe from beside him and disappeared behind the rock. She came out dressed in her robe and headscarf. She set Ajay's folded shirt on the ground beside him.

"Considering we may not reach the border town," Ajay said, "I feel obliged to tell you the truth. I stole my drums. Stole them from the very man who loaned them to me and taught me how to play." The man had been a music professor where Ajay worked as a janitor. They chatted and without directly saying so, struck a deal. Ajay would be the humble beggar and the teacher would feel superior for dispensing charity.

Ajay stood and grabbed his T-shirt. He lifted the material to his nose and inhaled the scent of dust and body oil. Her dust, her oil. He drew the shirt over his head and ran a hand from belly to waist, smoothing the cloth. He liked being inside where she'd been.

"And I'll tell you something, a secret," he said. "My drums are the hiding place of my heart. I'm telling you this because if I die — say because someone gets me lost and I run out of food and water — my heart will live on. Clever, yes?"

He smiled, but Madina didn't. She nodded. Like the joke hadn't been a joke and she understood far more than Ajay had meant to convey.

The wind pummeled Ajay from all sides. He and Madina crouched in a narrow ravine of acacia trees in a barren valley on this,

45

the dusk of their fourth day in the desert. There were no phone lines, no roads, no border towns, no mountain ranges.

"It looks like rain," Ajay yelled above the roar.

A black army of clouds raged overhead, altering the light of evening and making the gray rock almost black. Wind funneled dust into snakes writhing upward. Lightning forked to the ground, followed by the crackle and boom of thunder that echoed off a rock wall kilometers away. Madina continued her search for a hidden spring. She'd told Ajay this was a dry riverbed and there should be water beneath the surface. Look at the trees, she'd said. Trees meant water somewhere. Rain would mean water, too, but how could they collect it? If only they had a bowl or bucket.

But they didn't. Ajay sat and yanked off his boots and pulled out their tongues to widen each opening. Then he ran to the almost empty waterskin and laid the bag on the ground, the coin-sized opening toward the sky. He retrieved his three water bottles, two of plastic and one of glass, opened their tops and screwed the bottoms into the sand. But after being forced only a few centimeters beneath the surface, the bottles hit rock. The moment Ajay took his hands off the plastic vessels, the wind rolled them away. Ajay ran to catch them.

An explosion of lightning sent Ajay to the ground, arms over his head. He raised his eyes and saw Madina on her knees, pawing at the ground near the base of a gnarled tree, strands of hair whipping about her head. Another web of lightning spanned the sky, nearer this time, followed by a jagged crack of thunder.

Madina cried out, a strangle deep in her throat. Ajay ran in a low crouch against the wind to where she sat back on her heels before the hole, which was dry.

Ajay pointed to the sky. "Look! At any moment it'll rain—"

The lightning cracked again. The reflected streak split the darkness in her heated eyes.

CHAPTER 7

The branches of the bleached tree resembled bone claws against a sapphire sky of oncoming night. The sun had set and as the remaining light bled away, the trunk grew paler until becoming white tinged with the blue hue of shallow water. Water, of which Madina and Ajay had almost none. They sat on the sand.

Ajay shivered despite his sweater and the blanket around him. His eyelids felt heavy and his throat swollen. His lips hurt when he moved them. Even if they had food, he doubted he could eat. Madina sat on his left, staring into the distance. She, too, was shaking from the cold wind.

"I don't mean to disrespect your friends, but I'm sick of the wind," Ajay said, his voice a scratch. "Say that in English for me. 'I am so sick of the wind.'"

"I am no sick of the wind," Madina said in English.

Ajay opened his mouth to correct her — not *no*, but *so* — then closed his mouth. She knew what she'd said.

"It's *not*," Ajay said. He pulled the blanket tight around him. 'I am *not* sick of the wind.' And I'll tell you something. You're too loyal. There is such a thing as being too loyal. Too much loyalty can lead you into a trap. Kill you."

Madina said nothing.

He'd taught her English words all day yesterday and all day today on this, their fifth day in the desert. Their last. Maybe even

47

their last on earth. Because that was what one did to keep from going crazy while walking next to someone who wouldn't stop and didn't seem to understand the direness of the situation. Madina looked as beaten — as dirty — as Ajay yet somehow continued a steady pace. Where did she get the energy? The best Ajay could do was follow while forcing himself to think about nonsense. How buildings were constructed and the distance of stars and the skills one needed to weave a blanket. Any subject that didn't involve liquid of any kind, especially water, his thirst neither a desire nor a longing, but a lust so strong the craving kidnapped every cell in his body. If he stared at anything too long, the object quivered and waved before flowing, a river.

Again he shook his head. Again he told himself to think of something else. Like how for the past three nights Madina had screamed in her sleep. Nightmares horrific enough to reduce a woman impervious to fear to a whimpering baby, the sound hot and smothered. How had she survived those torments before he came along to help her nightmare-tortured mind slip into a safer realm?

"I was—" and Ajay coughed from the dust in his throat. "I was thinking. Maybe all this talk of revenge is a lie. Maybe the real reason the winds want to take over the world is because they want all the power. Maybe they're just as greedy as humans."

"They're not like people," Madina said.

The limbs of the tree had grown dark against the night sky. A finger of wind slipped down Ajay's back. He shook off the sensation, tugged open the flap of his pack and rummaged to the bottom. He located the book of matches from a hotel in Alexandria, stood and walked to the tree. A tree that had once been healthy and strong, but at some point had succumbed to the sun and wind. As Ajay and Madina might, even if she pretended otherwise. He struck a match and lit a branch then dipped the flaming tip into the hollows and crags of the tree, touching here, there. When ten little fires burned, Ajay lodged the stick in the tree's branches and stepped back. In the time necessary to bite and chew a piece of bread and wash it down with a swallow of water, fire consumed the dead wood with a crackling and popping that smacked liked satisfied lips.

"Eat well, fire," Ajay said.

Orange, yellow and blue encased the tree, sending sparks into the night, confetti that fell upward. The fire clicked and sputtered at the edges of an overall roar.

"Can you hear the wind talk?" Madina said. She sat on the ground, her knees drawn to her chest and eyes on the fire. "Through the flames. Can you hear it?"

Ajay listened. "I hear the hissing of sand blowing along the ground."

"Yes."

"What kind of wind is it?"

"A spy wind, I think."

"A spy wind? Sent by the evil wind to watch us die?"

"We're not going to die," she said. "You saw them, the mountains—"

"Shhh." Ajay lifted a finger to his lips. Then he whispered, "Maybe if we look pathetic and hopeless the spy wind will go back and report us as good as dead. Then maybe the evil winds will leave us alone and we'll have a chance to reach a town tomorrow." Ajay laughed a single *ha*, the sound no more than a puff of breath. He sat cross-legged beside Madina and allowed his eyes to ride the jagged profile of the mountain range in the distance beyond the engulfed tree. They might make civilization, and they might not, because those mountains were far yet, and he and Madina would consume the last of their water tonight. How many hours would they be able to go after that before their bodies shut down? Twenty-four, maybe?

Then again, if he and Madina did manage to reach a town in time, he would need to be ready. He opened the zippered pocket of his backpack and withdrew a square of yellow cloth that he unfolded on his lap. Within lay a round mirror the size of an egg along with a pair of nail scissors. Ajay held the mirror in his hand and turned sideways enough to catch the firelight. With his other hand he used the scissors to trim his mustache. He tilted his head to focus on the right side when he felt fingers take the mirror. He gazed up at Madina, who knelt before him, holding the mirror. Ajay put a finger beneath her elbow and lifted her arm a bit.

"There," he said. His fingertips lingered on the underside of her arm, flesh that shifted and flowed beneath his touch.

The tree fire raged, the smell of charred wood heavy in the air one moment and whisked away by wind the next. Ajay clipped, a

49

snip here, a snip there. The heat. Her gaze. Melding. He lifted his eyes to hers.

"How's that?" he said.

Madina lowered the mirror and studied his face from forehead to mouth and ear to ear. She reached a hand toward his face just like she reached for a rock to climb. Guided by feel and appreciating every contour. In his mind, he urged her on. A little more, just a little—

But her hand stopped. She pulled her fingers back. Ajay released a fraction of his held breath. A little at a time as opposed to a harsh sigh so she wouldn't know how she'd made his heart convulse. She handed him the mirror, turned and sat with her back to him.

Did Madina realize how she was luring and tempting him? Maybe Madina was not as crazy as imagined. More dangerous, yes. Leading him to believe his life would change soon, when that change wouldn't take place until he reached America, where his future belonged. The danger within Madina didn't stem from cunning, then, but from something worse: sincerity. Making him believe he had a place beside her and a good deed to accomplish, his first. How did a man avoid being sucked into such a fantasy – made to feel his every action mattered, when nothing he'd ever done before had mattered?

"Tell me," he said. "Tell me about your scar."

Madina lifted the flute to her lips. Ajay sat just a bit straighter. Was she going to play for him, after his repeated efforts to have her do so had failed? After she had said so many times that she did not play for people? Ajay closed his sore eyes. When the first notes came, he imagined laughing children who roughhoused and joked, skipped and yelled. Then the tone shifted, like a cloud covering the sun. The wind blew stronger. More clouds filled the air. The light became a thin film of gray and something happened, something disturbing.

Ajay cocked his head, the pulse of the low notes hypnotic and on the rise. A warning had been issued and the children had run home. He pictured a girl standing outside a door, banging and yelling. She was trying to warn the person inside that danger was coming. But the person inside couldn't hear. The danger turned the corner. The closer the menace came, the more chaotic the music grew until becoming a cacophony trebled by gusting sighs of wind. The music rose and rose and rose, then stopped.

Ajay jumped to his feet. Madina sat before him with eyes closed and brows furrowed, her mouth open in a grimace. She gripped the flute in both hands. Ajay wanted to yell. What happened to the girl? Did the danger catch her? What about the person inside? Ajay opened his mouth, ready to command that Madina play the answer. But before he could speak, Madina lifted the flute to her mouth again.

Ajay had wanted to think the girl and the person inside escaped. But the music. Rather than reflect a girl plucked from the path of rampage, the music limped along, lost, dazed. The girl and adult had been caught after all. Caught and pummeled. Ajay could feel the depth of the wounds. But the isolation was the most agonizing of all, a laceration that went untreated. The limping stopped and started, stopped and moved on again, Madina playing three notes and silencing the fourth. On the fifth repetition, Ajay understood. For every three breaths of catastrophe there was one of relief, because an end had come. The worst kind of end, but an end nonetheless.

The repetition grew to a steady climb of notes. The tune broadened, gained in confidence and leveled out on a high, whispered note that grew in volume. The notes flowed longer and farther until stretching out and disappearing into the distance.

Madina opened her eyes and lowered the flute, her face an orange fire. The wind circled inside Ajay's open mouth. He licked his lips and swallowed, his head throbbing. He placed a hand to his heart. To be surprised made one vulnerable and to be vulnerable was to be dead. Yet everything about her surprised him. Opened him. When the situation should be reversed.

"How do you do that? How do you... you – capture life and breathe it out. Everything there. The complexity, the variety of sound and abundance of color." He squatted before Madina. "Tell me," he said. "Tell me what you played."

"I can't."

"You have to."

"No."

"Yes!" Ajay jumped to his feet.

51

But Madina's face remained closed.

"You're like the rock you climb," Ajay said. He paced. He brushed his mustache, first one side and then the other, his movement fast, abrupt. A piece of cut hair fell onto his tongue and he spit it out. That a person could thieve her way into another's soul. A ribbon of wind slid over him. The wind. He stopped pacing. His face relaxed.

"Do you realize," he said, "that your Sister Wind wants you to tell me?"

Madina looked up at Ajay. "Why?" she said.

"Because your Sister Wind is a wind, and your breath is a type of wind," Ajay said. "You breathe in, you breathe out. Sometimes you breathe in good things and sometimes bad things. Sometimes when you breathe in those bad things, they stay inside and spoil."

"Like milk?"

"Right," Ajay said. He sat cross-legged before Madina. "Milk," he murmured, more to himself than to her. More to the child he once was. The force and deception waning, what he said more true than not.

"Spoiled milk," he said. "It can make you sick, just like bad things can make you sick. Can make you rot from the inside out. Your Sister Wind. She's good to you, yes? She'd want you to breathe out the bad wind."

Madina didn't move.

"Would it help if I play while you talk?" he said.

Madina nodded. Ajay set up his drums. He lifted his hands. When Madina spoke, he played.

"There was a girl," Madina said. "She was ten when her aunt took her away to the oasis. Ten when she wandered out into the desert and found the wall of rock."

The rock was smooth and pale and marred by jagged patches that made the girl think of scars.

"Scars like the one on the girl's face," Madina said.

Every day the scar pulled tighter, forcing the girl to smile when she had nothing to smile about. She was still weak from the infection that made her throw up and shake for ten days after the—

"—accident," Madina said.

The wind groaned. The burning tree crackled. Ajay played a slow, meditative rhythm for the scarred girl who stared up at the cliff. The girl would have rather died alongside her mother than endure what she felt now.

"Empty," Madina said. "Hollow. Like a camel carcass after everything has been scooped out. Because before the accident, the girl and her mother were happy. Most of the time. When the mother felt well." When she felt well, she and the girl would laugh and tell each other stories.

And when the mother didn't feel well?

"Then the girl would watch over her and wait," Madina said, "making sure her mother didn't hurt herself."

The girl would sit in a corner of their one room and watch her mother stare out the window or sleep, the day bleeding to night. During those silent hours, the daughter became acquainted with the winds that entered through the window, though the girl didn't understand yet what they were trying to tell her. All she knew was that they kept her company and helped her remain vigilant.

"On the night her mother died, the wind was warm and lovely," Madina said. "The air blew about the girl's neck and shoulders and pulled her forward, toward the door. The girl could almost hear the wind whisper, '*come outside, away for awhile.*'"

Ajay intensified the beat, urging the girl out the door, too.

But when the girl reached the door, she stopped—

Don't.

But she did anyway. She stopped and looked back at where her mother sat slumped in a corner, staring at the floor at some unseen horror, refusing to eat or drink.

Ajay's hands picked up speed.

Though the daughter had seen her mother through many of these spells, the girl had never seen one this dark.

Leave or she'll kill you.

But the girl shut her ears to the wind and stayed.

Ajay fell farther into the room with the mother and daughter, who fell against one another. Afterward, the aunt was there, and a doctor, too.

My niece, she fell on a stick, one sharp as a knife, I tell you! the aunt said in a loud whisper. The girl lay on a mat, the deep gash

53

on her face bandaged and her head banging. *My sister, the girl's mother, she was too young, too indulgent. She told the girl not to run with the stick, but the girl didn't listen. What a shame, for my niece would have been such a beauty. Like her mother had been.*

Had been, the girl thought. *Had been* meant something, though the girl wasn't sure what. *Had been*, as in *used to be*? But the girl couldn't think. Didn't know. Felt so hot she shivered. And how her face ached.

I should tell you, Doctor, that her mother couldn't take the shock. One moment to have a perfect little daughter, who would have one day found herself a wealthy husband, and the next to have a child scarred for life. Well, her mother couldn't take it. She felt responsible. She was a nervous woman, my sister. Not quite right in her mind. She must have felt so guilty. The aunt's voice grew weepy. *That's why my sister killed herself. Do you see?*

The girl tried to open her eyes. One lid flapped and fell shut. The other eye didn't open at all due to a heaviness, like a bag of sand sat on her eye. Why would someone put a bag of sand on her eye? And why did the aunt say that she *had* a beautiful sister who killed herself, when the aunt only had one sister, the girl's mother, and the girl's mother wasn't dead. But the words floated away.

I found the child there in the corner, shivering, blood all over her face and clothes. Just staring at her mother on the floor, dead. Terrible. So terrible.

The girl remembered opening her one eye long enough to see her mother lying on her side, head resting on her arm. A fly landed on her shoulder. She had to be asleep or she'd brush the fly away. The fly walked down her neck and across her cheek to her lip where the insect rubbed its front legs together. Why didn't the woman twitch? The girl stopped remembering because now she knew what *had been* meant. *Had been alive* and *was now dead*. The moment in which the girl turned into a ghost.

The aunt hustled the ghost onto a bus. They traveled for two days, during which the aunt whispered into the ghost's ear. *It's your fault your mother killed herself. You didn't listen to her. But you'll listen to me. You'll listen and you'll pay for the inconvenience you've caused me. You'll pay for your mother's death.*

The ghost didn't bother to tell her aunt what really happened.

And what really happened?

But Madina stopped, so Ajay stopped. They stared at one another, the wind licking Ajay's body, his numb hands resting on his drums. In his mind he listened to what sounded like a thousand years' of whining and wailing uttered by oceans of people who had grieved for what they lacked. Of food and clothes they didn't have and of love and comfort sought but never won. The color not right for this, the spices too bitter on the tongue. Having what they needed, yet claiming they had *waited too long for it.* Words uttered by people who knew nothing of real darkness. By people who equated inconvenience to starvation, and bruises to mortal wounds; people who lived every day with their hand out, not to give, but to receive. They talked and talked and took and took. Talk first then take, take, take.

But sometimes — rarely — there were people who, when asked to give, gave everything. No tears. No whimpers. People who understood what happened to them and knew they couldn't take back or redo. People like Madina, when Ajay had thought the opposite, that she was a blind woman who'd wrapped herself in another world to avoid the one she lived in. Yet she not only saw her past, but had committed to the future. Going on instead of giving up. Her strength a power hard to fathom. A strength that grew from her belief in the wind, which had saved her life, a debt Madina repaid with loyalty, unshakeable and absolute.

Madina watched Ajay. Maybe waiting for him to say something, and maybe some day he would. Maybe some day he'd tell her she was the one who saved herself, and on that day her crushing burden would turn to feathers and fly away on the wind she loved. And on that day, too, maybe he would understand how a person could willingly endanger herself for the sake of another.

But until that day came, Ajay understood what he, an accomplished thief, would do. He'd steal her winds from her. Her lunacy thieved, sanity would take its place. That was how he'd repay her for delivering him from the desert into the safety of Morocco.

The tree had been reduced to black limbs and a glowing ember trunk that simmered and popped as the night wind carried the last of their music away.

CHAPTER 8

The border town at the base of the mountain range leading into Morocco was still a distance of two, maybe three kilometers. Ajay wore a scarf over his nose and mouth to conserve body moisture, an idea Madina had suggested. A rock bounced off his boot into the rubble that extended for miles on either side of the two-lane road. Ragged clouds of thin white stretched across the pale mid-morning sky.

The wind pushed Ajay and Madina from behind. Toward a war instead of away from one. Ajay smiled, a slight curve of his mouth, despite the dizziness due to heat and lethargy from lack of water. Such privation squashed one's ability to think, to plan. While every step brought him closer to survival, the opportunity also meant risk. People, police and business transactions that could go wrong.

So many things to consider, yet all Ajay could think was *I — am — so — thirsty*, a word-per-stride mantra that filled his mind. His legs shook. His swollen tongue lolled in his mouth. His eyelids were coarse papers rubbed over rocks. He tried to forget his thirst, but the image came to mind, of a woman he once saw bathing herself in the Ganges, her orange and gold sari clinging to her skin while water dripped from her lips. The river flowed around her waist and away, a band of water over a thousand kilometers long in either direction.

Ajay stared into the distance. Heat undulations made the town glimmer and ripple. The community consisted of mostly single-story, flat-topped buildings awash in dirty pastels. In the midst of the buildings rose a minaret, a slender white tower with dark, open arches at the top. Though unimpressive, the town was many times bigger than Madina's oasis, and more importantly, possibly big enough to do business without attracting attention.

And then there were the trees. Hundreds, perhaps thousands, of date palms growing throughout the settlement. Many more were planted in neat rows in a date grove to the east. Ajay started to lick his cracked lip, tongue in the corner of his mouth, then stopped. He scanned the voluptuous, blowing tree fronds, so cool and dry and maddeningly adapted to this inferno. Like Madina.

She carried her pouch in one arm and with the other hand, veiled the lower half of her face with a corner of her scarf. She didn't strike him as a devout Muslim, greatly concerned with the observation of the behavioral rules of her religion. Therefore she either knew the importance of playing along or she didn't want anyone to see her scar. Either way, her instinct to cover up would be to their advantage. If the town were inhabited by religious tyrants suspicious of lone women, Madina would draw less attention with Ajay at her side. In turn, he would be less conspicuous with a female in tow.

"I've been thinking," Ajay said. "When we get to town, we should pretend to be husband and wife."

He kept his eyes on the road. She'd be nervous, but too bad. She'd fulfilled her promise, though barely, and led them out of the desert. Now Ajay was in charge.

First they'd get water. Then he'd arrange transportation out of town. There'd be police, so he'd have to find out how many, where they were and if they were looking for him. Then he'd have to fix his visa situation. He could try bribery, but even such a standard procedure was not without risk. He'd have to use money instead of jewelry, the former less remarkable than the latter. With any luck he'd find a healthy black market in which to sell the jewelry and trade his few *dinar* into *dirham*.

He and Madina passed a one-story compound with a huge antenna on the flat roof. They passed more outlying houses and then neared businesses on either side of a dirt street six or seven blocks long. Three veiled women in black walked in a group ahead. A thin-tailed dog scuttled out from the corner of a house and trotted sideways across the street. A man squatted, knees to chin, in front of a plain wooden doorway, reading a book spread on the ground. Three little boys ran up from behind. They circled Madina and Ajay. While the children seemed to peg Ajay as a foreigner, they looked unsure about Madina in her dusty robe and headscarf. Instead of asking for money, they dashed down the street.

Ajay watched Madina from the corner of his eyes. How she shifted her eyes right and left, right and left.

"It'll be all right," Ajay said.

Madina nodded, yet her eyes continued to shift.

Up ahead to the right, two men sat drinking and smoking at a few tables outside a cafe. A heavy tobacco smell on the dry air.

Ajay stopped outside the café. "Wait here."

Madina stared at him, eyes large, intent. He walked past the men and into the darkness.

There were five wooden tables. Three older men in various stages of baldness sat at the table closest to the front door. They stared at Ajay. At what he must look like, wild-haired, emaciated, crack-lipped. Ajay stood taller. He walked past them to the counter, behind which stood an old man shorter than Ajay and dressed in an off-white robe and skullcap. The hair of the man's eyebrows was so long the strands almost drooped into his black eyes.

"Water, please," Ajay said. A rasp.

The old man frowned. Yet he turned and poured water into a glass. Ajay reached for the glass, forcing himself not to grab. He would drink only a little so he wouldn't throw up. But once the glass met his lips, Ajay closed his eyes and drank, unable to stop. Streams of water slid from the corners of his mouth and down his neck. When done, he set the glass on the counter with a shaking hand. He caught his breath.

"More, please," he said.

The man stared at Ajay for a moment before picking up the empty pitcher and walking through a doorway into a back room. Ajay waited, the water a ball in his belly. He glanced out the café door to where Madina stood in the hot sun. She'd had nothing to drink for almost two days, yet she waited as he instructed. Ajay looked the other way. His eyes settled on the doorway through which the man had disappeared. A doorway that probably led to a kitchen, one with a back door out which a person could slip away. A hot breeze circled the room.

Yet her eyes. How they peered into the darkened interior of the cafe, trusting he was there even if she couldn't see him. A woman who had moved through the desert in queenly, owning strides, yet who now stood waiting. Like a dog. A woman who thought she could save mankind when nothing could save mankind.

The old man entered with a pitcher of water and refilled Ajay's glass. Ajay lifted the drink but stopped when he heard the flute. He whipped his eyes toward Madina. But she stood, one arm at her side, the other holding her pouch. Waiting, when her music had been so clear, the flow that of when she'd played the remainder of her story last night amid the dying embers of the ravaged tree. Of a girl on the floor, struggling with her mother, the girl's body shaking as she gripped her mother's wrist, the knife a pinky-length from the girl's left eye. A knife of wooden handle and nicked blade from years of everyday use. The girl's eyes darted from the knife to the mother's eyes, their brilliance emanating from the dark face surrounded by tangled hair. Eyes that saw a demon instead of a daughter.

Then the girl's arm gave out. She fell onto her back. The knife swooped forward. The girl grabbed her mother's wrist again, but too late. The blade pressed into the corner of the girl's left eye as she turned her face away, the skin flying open.

Ajay banged the bottom of the glass on the counter. Water sloshed onto his hand. Eyes turned toward him, their movement a flutter at the edge of his vision. He shook his head, but the music didn't go away.

He licked his trembling lips. "And another glass. For my wife."

The man's eyebrows rose and Ajay pointed out the café's front window to where Madina stood. The man shifted his eyes to Ajay and said nothing. He filled a second glass. Ajay slipped his drum bag over his wrist so he could carry a glass in each hand. He extended a hand toward Madina. She accepted what he gave. She dropped the corner of her scarf, tilted her head back, closed her eyes and drank.

Again a bead of water escaped her mouth, running a river down her neck. Ajay watched the drop soak into the cloth of her headscarf, causing a darkness to spread outward. Like blood from a wound in her throat. Madina handed Ajay her empty glass. He went back inside for more.

Each time Ajay returned to the café for a refill, he chatted with the café owner about the location of the bus and where he could find a food market. Necessary information that could also distract one from his thoughts of flies walking into the mouths of the dead. When Ajay returned to the counter for the last time, he smiled at the café owner.

"It was a long walk," Ajay said.

The old man stood with a fist on his hip, the other hand on the counter. "You were lost, weren't you, out there? You're lucky you two didn't die, your bones picked over by beetles. Maybe not such a good place for a wife."

Ajay said nothing.

The old man told Ajay to get his other water vessels. Ajay did, and when he left the café for the last time, his backpack was heavy with full bottles. He handed the waterskin to Madina, who hoisted the dripping bag over her shoulder. They continued down the street and passed a mechanic's shop, a store selling vegetables and spices, and a bus station. When they passed a restaurant with a picture of a smiling goat stenciled in black above the door, Ajay inhaled. Lamb kabob. His stomach growled.

"We'll eat soon," he said.

Madina said nothing. Her eyes roamed everywhere, this woman who'd never been anywhere but the oasis and where she was born. He started to smile. But in his mind he heard Old Aunt's voice, *"Girl!"* And the small room, the blue curtain blowing in the wind. For years. His smile fell away.

When they came to a tiny movie theater featuring a poster of an Arab man in battle, Ajay stopped. Maybe after he'd taken care of a few things, and if he had to wait awhile, he would go. He turned to Madina and found her studying a plump woman who walked with a slow hip-swish down the street, a basket of oranges on her head. The woman was dressed in a bright red skirt and white blouse and her chin was tattooed with a delicate dot design. A Berber. Ajay's eyes followed Madina's gaze to the woman's skirt. To the design or color, or maybe both. Apparently no woman above vanity.

61

They continued past a post office, police station and hotel. When Ajay spotted a bakery ahead, he led Madina to a bench outside the door and told her to wait. He had business to do and would be back soon.

He turned and looked up one side of the street and down the other. They couldn't eat until he got money and suddenly he had to eat. Was dying to eat, his stomach and mind wild for satiation. And just beneath that, the urgency to press on had returned, though keener this time, to the point of piercing.

"Wait," she said.

Ajay turned. Madina untied her pouch. He leaned forward to see what else she might keep in there besides the knife. But Madina kept an arm over the pouch. She withdrew her fist and opened her hand and there in her palm were five or six coins.

"They won't be any good in Morocco, true?" Madina said.

"True."

Madina lifted her hand to Ajay. "Can you exchange them for me?"

Ajay reached for the coins, his fingertips brushing her palm. He nodded. "I'll get you a good rate." He turned away, slipping the coins into his pocket. He surveyed the street, yet still he didn't go. He glanced back at her.

"Wait here," he said again.

He left.

Madina was still sitting on the wooden bench, her back against the warm, white stucco wall, when they came walking in her direction. An indigo robe covered the man's entire body and face, save for his eyes. His pregnant wife trailed behind him, her big belly wrapped in a black skirt, her head and shoulders draped in a scarf of blood red and white. The man's eyes skipped from one shop sign to the next. When he came to the bakery, only six strides from where Madina sat, he made a sharp turn through the wide, open doorway. His wife followed.

Once inside, the man asked the store owner a question. The store owner — also a man — answered. They were loud in what they said to one another. Madina cocked an ear in their direction.

CHAPTER 9

Ajay walked down the street, the bakery still a ways away. He held the purchases he'd made in both arms. Business had gone well. After making a few inquiries he'd acquired money, bought bus tickets and made a special arrangement with the bus driver. All this had taken only an hour. By this time tomorrow he and Madina would be well into the mountains, like snakes that had slipped through a hole just the right size. Ajay smiled at the late afternoon sun and rounded the corner of a building. He stopped. His smile disappeared. He stared at the empty bench in front of the bakery. He glanced up and down the street, but didn't see Madina.

He walked into the street to see farther down the road. He first checked the direction from which he and Madina had entered town. A car horn honked behind him, but Ajay didn't move. The driver pulled around Ajay and yelled curses in passing. But Ajay kept searching. He saw a man and woman walk out of the police station and a squat woman shake a rug while standing on a doorstep. But Ajay didn't see Madina.

He turned the other way, to where the road led out of town.

Up ahead, a small boy in black shorts jabbed the ground with a stick while walking alongside a man who led three camels toward the mountains in the distance. A boy, a man, three camels. And beyond them, someone walking away from him, without food, without money. Without anyone to lead her to safety.

Ajay adjusted the packages in his arms and walked fast. When he drew close to Madina, he wiped the anger from his face. He circled around and stopped in her path. Madina stopped, her lower face covered by the scarf, her eyes startled. The boy, man and camels passed.

"Going somewhere?" Ajay said.

"To the mountains," she said.

"Ah," Ajay said. "So you've picked a direction in which to proceed, one you think will bring you closer to this war, no doubt. How did you make your choice?"

"The baker –"

"The baker! Of course. The baker knows all."

Madina dropped her eyes.

Ajay scratched his nose on his shoulder and shrugged to get a better grip on everything he carried.

"What about the baker? He must have said something important, to get you to leave without any provisions."

"He didn't really say anything," Madina mumbled. "He was yelling. He told them they didn't have enough money—"

"Told who?"

"A man and woman," Madina said. "They were in his shop. They didn't have enough to pay, so he told them to go back to the mountains."

Ajay waited for further explanations, but Madina was silent.

"That's it?" Ajay said. "The baker threw people out of his shop, told them to go back to the mountains and you decided that's where you're supposed to go?"

Madina nodded. Ajay rolled his tongue around his cheek.

"Something else happened, didn't it?" he said.

Her eyes set upon him, their intensity as sharp as last night, in the desert.

"Here," Ajay said. He rebalanced the items in his arms to free a hand and led her by the elbow to an alley. He nodded for her to sit on an empty crate and then set down his bundles and drum bag and squatted before her. Still she held the scarf over her face. He reached forward and rested his fingertips on her hand. The hand slowly lowered, revealing her face. Lips, nose, scar.

"Tell me what happened," he said.

"My Sister Wind—"

"I thought it couldn't come this far."

"It was very risky for her, but she wanted to warn me."

"About what?"

"That a wind will try to change me."

"Which one?"

"I don't know."

"Change you how?"

"I'm not sure."

"Change you for the worse?"

"Yes."

Ajay dropped his eyes to the ground and rubbed the back of his neck. A beetle scuttled up one side of his boot and down the other. At least Madina hadn't meant to abandon him. Yet that kind of irrational impulsivity would make helping her harder than expected. Today Madina had been affected by the offhand remark of a stranger. Tomorrow she might find meaning in a strange shadow and the next, a bird flying overhead or the color of a skirt, until she had him running in circles.

Ajay cleared his throat and sharpened his tone. "You said this wind would try to change you. Do you want to change?"

"No."

"Then you won't. I don't believe people ever really change, they only think they do." He held her gaze for a moment more, then jumped to his feet.

"I bought us something to eat," he said and unwrapped one newspaper bundle to reveal two skewered kabobs. "With cabbage and carrots." He handed her one. Madina grasped the skewer with a trembling hand, and began to devour the food.

"I bought couscous, too, and honey cakes," Ajay said. "I tried to get a bargain on the oranges, but the woman, she was a camel." Ajay shrugged off his backpack and opened the sack for Madina to see.

"And look at these," he said. He opened the brown package and unfurled a bright blue skirt covered in fist-sized white flowers. He flung the cloth out and let the material drift down onto Madina's lap. Then he pulled out a red blouse splashed with other colors.

Yellow, green, gold, purple. He held the blouse against his own chest for her inspection.

Madina's chewing slowed as her eyes moved from the skirt in her lap to the blouse to Ajay. She swallowed. "Who are they for?"

Ajay laughed. "For you."

"To wear?"

"Of course to wear!" he said. "They'll look good against your skin, the colors."

When Madina said nothing, Ajay pointed at the clothes she was wearing. "Look at you now. You have no color on you. Color is good. It livens things up. I like color. Bright colors. I saw a yellow there in the store that I liked, but I had to choose and I liked these better."

Ajay laid the blouse on Madina's lap. She raised her hand that held the kabob so the cloth wouldn't brush against it. She stared at the new clothes, her face a whirlpool of wonder. So young. So different than last night when she told him the rest of her story, what her aunt hadn't seen and didn't know. A confession confessed as sparks flew, whisked away by a wind sailing ragged clouds across a white moon. While Ajay had played a slow rhythm of bare existence on his drums to mirror the rock of Madina's demeanor.

And now here she was, overwhelmed by something as simple as a piece of cloth.

Ajay smiled. "Life can be good, yes?"

Madina nodded.

He began to devour his own kabob. He had been able to delay eating while talking to Madina only because he had already had a few bites to eat before he rejoined her. They both finished the kabobs quickly and then began on the couscous, washing everything down with huge quantities of water from the bottles.

When they were through eating Ajay wiped his mouth with the back of his hand. Then he snapped his fingers, as if remembering something. "How are you planning to cross the mountains?"

"Walk."

"Well, you could, though if you did, it would take a long time and you might miss the war of winds." He leaned down, rummaged in his backpack and pulled out two bus tickets. He leaned forward. "Though I should warn you I got them at a discount. We can't board until we're down the road a ways." Once outside the town, they would take a detour through the desert, rejoin the road and wait for the bus. "We'll have to walk a bit. We'll start tonight when the sun goes down."

Madina studied the tickets, then Ajay, with an eye that slanted down and a mouth that curled up.

"They're bus tickets," Ajay said.

"I know," Madina said. In English.

Ajay's face stilled. At her apparent ease in speaking a language he thought she didn't know beyond what he'd taught her as they walked through the desert. *How are you? I am fine, thank you.* And at his apparent mistake of underestimation, the type of error that could get a person into serious trouble.

Ajay nodded at the tickets. "Your Sister Wind and I chatted for awhile before she left. I told her which way I was going and she told me you had to cross the mountains, too, so—"

"You don't believe in the winds," Madina said.

Ajay stopped. After a moment he shrugged. "So? You believe. Isn't that what's important? And didn't Sister Wind tell you I was supposed to go with you?"

"Yes."

"Then why did you leave without me?"

Madina rolled her lower lip under, locking her mouth closed. A gust of wind through the alley flared the scarf, a billow of off-white. She shook her head, no.

If she hadn't forgotten then she meant to leave him. But why would she disobey her Sister Wind, the only being she trusted and for which she was willing to die? Did Madina dislike Ajay that much? If so, why had she been willing to wait in the burning sun for him, her flute in hand?

"Look," Ajay said. "I'm going through the mountains. I thought you might want to go, too."

"I'm sorry," she said.

Ajay frowned. "You don't want to go with me?"

"I do, but I—" She cast her eyes around, as if looking somewhere for an answer. "Thank you," she finally said, again in English.

Ajay sniffed, unable to remember the last time anyone had

thanked him. The last time he'd done anything to be thanked for. He shoved his hands into his pockets, trying to understand something at the edge of his understanding, something important. His fingertips touched the coins.

"I almost forgot. Here's your money," and Ajay pulled his hand out of his pocket and dropped the newly exchanged Moroccan money into her lap, releasing a few extra coins, too.

Part II

Utrukiini.

Leave me alone.

CHAPTER 10

The Atlas Mountains

The bus through the Atlas Mountains was really a van and nothing like the luxury liners tourists took. The rattling red box had a stubby nose, dinged sides and no air conditioning. The occupants had gotten on in the border town, so that when the bus stopped for Madina and Ajay, twenty people stuffed the main compartment, a space only big enough for twelve. Madina and Ajay had to ride on benches lashed to the roof, along with five other people and a crate of four small goats. The driver had wound higher into the mountains until dusk and stopped at a small mountain village where Madina and Ajay had slept on the ground, the air much colder than the desert. Ajay woke up exhausted from drifting in and out of sleep on the edge of a shiver.

The bus had only been on the road for three hours that morning when the engine belched black smoke that grew to a continuous spew. The driver crawled the vehicle along the road until reaching this Berber village where the bus was being repaired. Ajay and Madina were headed toward the enclave's only tourist attraction, an old *casbah* from which soldiers had guarded the town for centuries.

The village had been built on the side of a mountain. The streets were narrow and the two- and three-story buildings on either side made of pitted stone were so old the surface was stained with tears of gray, blue and green from centuries of rain and sun.

Electrical wires hung outside the buildings, which had narrow windows and walls that cast cooling shadows on the street.

The close, tall buildings and thin streets funneled the mountain wind into a strong current that barreled down the street. Ajay leaned into the wind, which smelled of lemon, manure and damp stone. Rain must have fallen and what he wouldn't give to feel moisture on his skin, to take a bath and free himself of dust.

"After being so long in the open, I don't like cities anymore," Ajay said.

Madina walked beside him, holding the scarf across her face.

"I'm from a big city in India, did I ever tell you that?" Ajay said. "It's like a sea compared to this," and he threw out a hand. "You could walk all day and never come to its shores."

Two women talked and laughed while walking toward Madina and Ajay on the opposite side of the street. The younger had her arms clasped behind her back while the older one walked with a stiff-hipped gait. Neither wore a head covering and both were dressed in sandals and worn, though still colorful, blouses and skirts of yellow, blue and black like the skirt Ajay had bought Madina. An item that had disappeared into Madina's pouch with no further mention.

As the women passed, Madina's eyes followed them with a look. The look. Ever on the prowl for the next clue about where to go in this search for her war.

A goat trotted around the same corner from which the women had appeared. The animal stopped and stared at Ajay, then trotted toward him. But when the goat came close, the animal veered to Madina and took her robe in its mouth and tugged. Ajay put his foot to the goat's barrel side and shoved the animal away. The goat scampered off, tail switching back and forth.

When Ajay returned his gaze to Madina, his glance turned into a stare. Not only had she dropped the veil from her face, but she'd also pulled off the headscarf, which now rested around her shoulders. The change sudden and somehow more revealing than nakedness, her hair blacker, thicker and curlier than he remembered.

Hair that made a person want to reach out and put his hand in the current of what looked like a silky, slow-moving river.

A loud group of ten to fifteen women came toward Ajay and Madina. Two women, then a goat and now this gaggle of females, trouble coming in triplets. The group approached, full of laughter and color, a celebration party of some kind. There were young women and old women and all of them walked with bobbing heads and flapping hands, their bright robes flowing after them like waves. Some of the women were linked arm in arm or arm around waist. Heavy silver jewelry jangled from around their necks and atop headdresses of braided rope, eyeball-sized metal bead necklaces around their necks. He stepped back to allow the women to pass.

"Do you think they get headaches from wearing all that on their heads?" Ajay said.

"It's a wedding," Madina said.

"Ah," Ajay said. A good reason for such heaviness.

"I wonder which one is the bride," Madina said.

The group passed and in the rear, an old man trailed behind the group. He had a large, hooked nose and was dressed in a long striped robe with a turban around his head, a beard across his face and a black cane that acted like a third leg. Though he hobbled fast to keep up with the group, the gap between them widened.

"The goat herder is losing his flock," Ajay said, smiling.

"What does your future bride look like?" Madina said.

Ajay kept his eyes on the retreating group. A direct question, a personal question, when she'd never asked either before.

"I don't know," he said. "It's an arranged marriage. I haven't even met her."

"Do you have a photograph?"

"No."

"Not even a photograph." But her tone was neither disbelieving nor sad. Ajay cut her a sharp glance. But she wasn't looking at him. She was looking at the sky, hands out, palms up.

"Do you feel it?" she said.

"Feel what?"

Madina pointed to the wedding party, now far up the street. The wind got beneath a woman's skirt and puffed out the fabric. She swished her hips forward and threw her arms to her sides to squash

73

the clothing. The women around her exploded with laughter. Even the older man laughed. Then the wind got beneath his robe and bloated him into a striped tube. He beat his robe with his cane and the cloth deflated at the same moment a heavy woman with short legs screamed, her skirt billowing out, too, to reveal fat knees. The other women shrieked and pummeled her skirt. The party turned a corner and disappeared.

Madina smiled, her lips open to reveal straight white teeth. A smile of joy Ajay had never seen before. A smile of joy on a face so recently imprisoned, and now freed. And the loosing of her hair — so much blackness — making her skin gold and her eyes pale. Her robe inflated and rather than beat the clothing like the old man had done, she watched the robe surge around her. Her brows rocketed in surprise and she stomped her foot.

"And what was that wind?" he said.

"A Joker Wind," she said.

"Ha," Ajay said. "A joker wind. And did this joker wind get a little too friendly with you?"

Madina glanced at him, then away. Smiling. Ajay laughed. Though the wedding party had disappeared around a corner, she continued to look after them, her smile dimming.

"A Joker Wind is better than a Lulling Breeze," she said.

"Let me guess. A wind that lulls a person?"

Madina turned and continued in the direction of the *casbah*. Ajay followed.

"My Sister Wind says it's the most beautiful wind of all," Madina said. "Light, gentle, soothing."

"So, why is a joker wind better than that? Is too much pleasure a bad thing?"

"No. It's— It's that it uses it's gentleness to get close to people. Then it steals their life."

"It kills them?"

"Only the weak. The very old, the very young, the sick. But that's if you're lucky."

"What do you mean?"

Madina walked. Ajay put his hand on her forearm. She stopped.

"What do you mean?" he said.

Her smile, the joy, the laughter. They were all gone. "If you're unlucky, the Lulling Breeze steals your soul, but leaves you alive."

Ajay shivered, then scoffed, the sound echoing against the stone buildings on either side. "I think your Sister Wind was just trying to scare you. Let's just go see this stupid *casbah*. Maybe by the time we get back the bus will actually be fixed." Wind crawled up his pants. He stamped his foot and walked on.

Ajay climbed the worn red clay steps of the exterior stairway leading to the rooftop terrace of the mountain fort. While he'd gone to tour the compound, Madina had remained on the rooftop to enjoy the view of the village below and the higher mountain peaks above. But now they needed to get back. The bus had to be repaired by now. If he and Madina were late, the bus driver would no doubt clatter off without them.

As Ajay neared the rooftop, he heard music. Not just music, but her music. A melody barely audible beneath the rush of wind down the staircase. And she had said she never played in public. Ajay took the steps two at a time and stopped near the top in the shadow of the staircase wall. Whereas Madina seemed to prefer slower, discordant tunes, this music ran rapid and harsh with energy. Ajay took the last few steps and emerged onto the roof, which was surrounded by a waist-high wall. Due to the late afternoon sun, the red clay of the building had turned a deep orange.

At the far end of the roof Madina sat cross-legged, sideways to Ajay and a man stood over her, seeming to study her as one would a sculpture. Her music ended with a sudden shriek. The man extended his hand and dropped something that flashed as it fell through the sunlight and into her lap. Then the man turned and walked toward Ajay. The man had a white beard and round belly and wore an intricately embroidered robe and a leather pouch over one shoulder. When he neared, he glanced at Ajay. A brief touching of eyes, yet filled with the man's disturbance. The man went down the stairs.

When Ajay turned his eyes back on Madina, she stood facing him, a dark figure outlined by a sinking sun. Her hair flew everywhere, tentacles about her head.

"I thought you didn't play for people," Ajay said, as he approached her.

"I didn't mean to. I was playing to the winds, and he came along.

"Tell me something," she said, her tone harsh and loud above the sudden gust of wind. "Do you think all people have the ability to kill other people?"

Ajay walked past her to the wall. He set down his drum bag and sat down beside it with his back against the wall.

"You mean besides to defend oneself?" he said. "As in out of greed, lust, jealousy, rage? Of course."

"Everybody?"

He crossed his ankles. "By which you mean you. Of course you. You, me, everyone can kill, given the right reason or cause."

Madina chewed on her lower lip and walked to the wall next to Ajay. She gazed at the ground three stories below. Where a few tourists walked. Where cars moved. Where goats grazed the hillside, the wind smelling of almond groves, junipers and the occasional drift of simmering food. Though all of that seemed very far away.

"Here's a true story for you," Ajay said in English.

"In Arabic."

"No." Ajay considered the darkening mountains. He wanted to find out, once and for all, how much English she knew. "When I was smaller, I happened to be along the river one night."

"Slower," she said.

Ajay continued at the same pace, still in English. "I saw a man," he said. "He was walking with a crying baby crooked in his arm, like a parcel." Ajay stood, strode five paces and turned to Madina. He crooked his arm to illustrate. "He walked under the bridge. Soon after, I heard a splash. The man came out from under the bridge. No baby."

"How terrible."

Ajay raised his hands. "He had a problem and took care of it." He fixed his eyes on Madina. "That's what people do. They decide to do something, then give themselves reasons for doing what they want."

But Madina didn't blink. Nor had she asked him to pause

while telling the rest of the story, her English apparently fluent. Ajay sat on the wall beside her.

"Has another wind been bothering you?" Ajay said in Arabic.

Madina nodded. "Ghost winds. They hover around this place, low along the ground."

Ajay stared at the rooftop below his feet. A terrace on which soldiers had walked and used weapons against intruders and in turn, been wounded or died, their blood seeping into the walls.

"What are those winds doing here?" Ajay said.

Madina remained silent. Ajay hopped off the wall and stood before her.

She tilted her head and considered him. "You get upset when I talk about the winds."

"I don't—"

"I can feel it. You think I'm crazy like my mother and these winds I hear are like the voices in her head."

"Well, there *is* a certain similarity," Ajay said.

Madina gazed to the right, toward the village.

"Then again," Ajay said, "I don't know everything. Your wind theories could be true. But I was born to doubt, just like you were born to believe. Some people doubt, some believe." He crossed his arms. "Now tell me about these ghost winds."

Madina swept her eyes over the rooftop and told him about winds that start as Land Lovers that lust for the smell of death.

"—and when they find a place where the smell is strong — a place like this — they stay. And because they refuse to move — to keep themselves vital — they die, only they don't know it."

"What have these ghost winds told you?"

"That I'm capable of killing."

"But you already know that."

She stood fast, her fists clenched again. "That was different." She looked away. A woman who'd already killed one person and seemed to think the day was coming when she'd have to kill another. Her and her fisted hands that knew the feel of a knife entering flesh, just as her ears knew the sound of a final breath and her eyes of how life could dim and disappear, a moment in which one *knew* reality, as opposed to knowing *of it*.

The wind carried the smell of a cooking fire. A veil of moon hung high in the early evening sky. Ajay drummed on his leg, then stopped.

"That's what you think, isn't it?" he said. "That the evil winds are trying to recruit you. To get you on their side. Then when the time comes, instead of stopping the war, you'll start it."

Madina looked down.

Ajay slipped his hands into the pockets of his worn pants and inhaled deeply. He gazed at the snowy peak above the village.

"You shouldn't be afraid of what you know," Ajay said. "It's what you don't know that will ambush you."

Yet she wouldn't look at him. The dying sun on her face, the wind blowing her hair back. The anguish.

"Besides," he said, "the winds couldn't destroy all of us. We're too small, too fast. Some of us would wriggle away and hide until it was safe to come out. Now come, it's late."

"Here, take this," Madina said. She lifted her right hand and waited. Ajay opened his palm beneath her fist and she dropped some coins into his hand.

"Is it enough to pay for a *tajine* and a lemon tart?" she asked. "One for you and one for me?"

"Yes," he said, the wind about his ankles like a swarm of rats.

CHAPTER 11

The mountain waterfall rose about six meters above a deep pool that drained into a stream. Ajay sat on the gravel ground by the pool, arms locked around his knees. Boys climbed the steep path of rocks to the top of the waterfall then one by one, jumped. They were probably all local boys, because when they jumped they did so with an abandon and fearlessness that only repetition could bring. Some of them flung their arms overhead and twisted, while others fell feet first with arms at their sides. Most yelled all the way down.

Ajay wiped his forehead on his sleeve. Though Madina sat beside him, he didn't look at her. The bus should have arrived in Marrakech this afternoon. Now they might not get there until tomorrow. All this wasted time, yet no one else seemed to care. Mothers from the bus, dressed in robes and veils, watched their skinny, bare-chested boys jump from the waterfall. Screaming warnings even as they laughed. Beside them sat wrapped-up daughters who could do nothing but watch or write messages in the damp earth. Most of the men talked in small groups and smoked. A young European couple — both thin, tall and blond — climbed after the boys and jumped.

Ajay stood and whipped a pebble into the water with a downward, slicing motion, then another. He walked to the water where he squatted and splashed water onto his face, neck and head. He stood, his hair dripping and eyes on those jumping through the air, free.

"*Bakvas,*" he whispered.

The European man jumped, his T-shirt flying upward to reveal a white belly.

Ajay yanked the laces of his boots, pulled them off and stood. He looked down at her, his eyes on hers. Even so, he could see, at the edge of his vision, the blue flowered skirt and the red blouse she wore, the clothes he'd bought her and she'd hidden away. Until today.

He pointed his finger at her. "Watch my drums," he said. "I trust no one with my drums. Not even you. If you ever see me without my drums, you know something bad has happened."

"What about now?" Madina said.

"Something bad has happened." Ajay turned away from her. "I've lost my self control."

He jogged toward the path and followed the dripping, hopping boys. Ajay gripped at the branches on either side of the path to pull himself up where the trail steepened. He concentrated on every step he took, but all he could see was the blue and white skirt and red blouse. He gritted his teeth and raised his eyes to the top of the waterfall, so close now. Sweat burned his eyes. He climbed.

"*Bakvas,*" he said, though louder this time. Because of the story Madina told him last night, of exactly how the winds could devastate the world, an image so vivid he couldn't sleep. And because when the bus driver had stopped this morning near a grouping of trees, Madina had gone off with the other women, presumably to relieve herself, and returned wearing the new clothes. A skirt that swung just above her slender ankles. A blouse that outlined her breasts. Rather than proving a hideous contrast to the joyful color, her scar seemed to fit the boldness of her thick hair and new attire. She walked to the bus with her pouch in her arm, her face calm, as though she'd dressed like that every day of her life. And then she smiled at him. Not a seductive smile or a shy smile or an amused smile, just a smile. Only when he sat next to her on the bus did he notice the gold bangle she wore around her right wrist. Like a married woman from India.

Madina, who might have plunged the knife into her mother's body, or not. Who might have been born somewhere other than the oasis, or not. Who might have invented the crazed mother to escape the cooking, cleaning, whoring. A loneliness so complete she'd conjured a fantasy of winds in which she was the savior of the world, this harmless, amusing, easily-led woman who every hour seemed to grow stronger, keener of eye. Leaving the path he'd set. The farther she diverged, the stronger his urge became, to follow and bring her back. To steal her away from her winds. Yet the farther out he went, the harder it would be to return.

Ajay breathed hard. He climbed the last few steps. He followed a boy who ran ahead, threw his arms in the air and jumped over the edge. Laughter erupted far below. Ajay neared the cliff edge, wanting it all to go away. Her black hair that he hadn't touched. Her slender calves that curved up underneath her skirt. Her music that remained in his head along with the stories she told. Her thin ankles, her lips, the scar her mother carved, or not. Though what burned most was the image of a ten-year-old girl standing at the edge of a cliff like this one, only higher, and there was no water below to break her fall. Ready to jump when at the last moment, a wind wrapped its arms around her and wouldn't let go.

Ajay looked over the edge. The boys behind him yelled to *jump, jump*. He turned, walked back five paces and again faced the cliff, his heart drumming. Ajay ran and yowled and threw his arms in the air, stretching the jump as far as possible. He felt the ground leave him.

The world became a downward rush. Instead of falling feet first, Ajay felt his body tilt forward. He flailed his arms, trying to push himself upright, but his body only pitched forward more until his belly flattened out, parallel to the pool's surface. The air streamed into his face. He thrashed his arms harder, his feet wilder. Body splayed, he hit the water.

CHAPTER 12

He lay on the mattress, hard and sunken beneath him. He opened his eyes. The small room in a village clinic not far from the waterfall. Madina sat on the edge of his bed.

"The old bus couldn't be fixed," Madina whispered. "A new one came and now it's ready to leave."

Ajay's head pulsed in a nonstop rhythm that clashed with the sudden streaks of pain that shocked through him every time he moved, the result of his two cracked ribs. A dull, warbling throb from his twisted left ankle provided a third, awkward rhythm, so that together, the music of his pain beat loud and discordant.

He turned his eyes away from her, but still there was her scent. Of a desert tree, dry, dusty, slightly bitter. A groan escaped his throat. He clamped his lips shut.

"Don't tell me I shouldn't have jumped," he said, his voice hoarse and faint.

"I won't," she said.

"Good."

The driver called. That everyone should come because the bus was leaving. Ajay closed his eyes.

"They're leaving," she said.

Ajay remained still. The bus, those people, driving away with their desires and destinations, bangles and pouches.

Ajay heaved himself up. He hissed, his arms hugging his bare chest. He drew his knees up, his eyes shut tight.

"My drums," he whispered.

"They are right here, on the floor," Madina said.

He panted a moment. "Don't tell me I shouldn't have jumped."

"All right."

Someone entered. He opened his eyes to see an old Berber woman in a bright yellow skirt, her body short and crooked as a gnarled acacia. She brought a cup to his lips and he sipped the tea. Her silver bracelets clinked.

"There is no such thing as love," Ajay told the woman.

The woman leaned over and whispered to Madina. Madina nodded. The woman left.

"And?" Ajay said.

"She said you should breathe deeply," Madina said.

Ajay tried to inhale, but stopped, his teeth bared. He exhaled over the course of many seconds.

"No such thing as love," he whispered between shallow breaths. "Only illusion."

"You should put your shirt on," Madina said. "It's getting cold." She reached to the small wooden table beside his bed and with both hands, offered him his T-shirt. But Ajay remained still. Madina lowered the shirt to her lap.

"You think a wind tried to kill me, don't you?" he said. "That it pushed me over the edge. Made me fall flat."

Madina said nothing.

"Well here's the truth. No wind tried to kill me. Do you hear? I fell because I let myself get distracted, and in this world— But you know about this world, don't you? That you either keep your wits about you or you die doing something stupid. I got distracted. I jumped. The wind gusted at the wrong moment. That's all."

"I—"

"Now I have a story for you before you leave," Ajay said, his mouth tight. "There once were a girl and boy who lived in a small village in the hills."

"The bus—"

"They seemed to belong together," Ajay said, "even as children. They played together. They shared secrets. Their parents knew one another. The elders of the village would nod their heads and say, 'Some day those two will marry.'"

Madina shifted forward to rise, but Ajay locked a hand around her wrist, the rumbling of the bus's engine roaring in his ears.

"So when the couple arrived at the proper age," Ajay said, "they were married and the whole village danced." He coughed and panted, feeling the skin stretch tight across his ribs. Almost breathless, he said, "The couple lived out a long and happy life until one day the man, now old and gray, went fishing as he normally did on the bridge above the river. Suddenly a bull with sharp horns came running across the bridge and the man had no choice but to jump in the river or be gored."

"Did he hit the water belly first?" Madina said.

Ajay smiled. "Unfortunately, no. Instead, what came along was a large fish looking for a meal. The fish swallowed the man and spit out his bones on the riverbank."

The bus driver yelled. A last call. Though Ajay gripped Madina's wrist tighter, she peeled his fingers away, and easily, too, like one might a tangerine. She stood. His T-shirt fell from her lap onto the floor.

"The old lady," Ajay said louder, his words faster, "was so filled with grief she cried and shrieked and tore her hair. Forty days she whined. The villagers got tired of listening and made her children take her to the village doctor."

Madina walked to the door, her pouch in her hand.

"I haven't finished," Ajay shouted, rising to his elbow and trying to stand. But Madina didn't look back. She walked out and closed the door behind her. And was gone. The bus driver gunned the engine.

Ajay took a swipe at his T-shirt on the floor and in the same motion, lodged his hand on the side table. He grimaced, sweat dripping down his face. He pushed himself to a sitting position and felt close to passing out. But he couldn't. He had to remain conscious. To think. Because he hadn't told her the whole story.

Ajay braced his forearm under his broken ribs. He threw his T-shirt over his shoulder. He lifted his boots by the shoelaces and clamped them between his teeth. With his free hand he lifted his backpack and drum bag, then dropped everything. The pain, the nausea. He closed his eyes and forced his breathing to slow. Then he stood, though this time he remained in a crouch and dragged his gear.

85

Ajay cursed through his teeth. He took his arm away from his chest long enough to open the door.

The Berber woman stood in the hallway with a jug of water riding on her wide hip. Rather than try and stop him, she watched him limp by, a smile on her wrinkled lips. He cursed her, though when he got to the front door, the Berber woman was there, waiting. Having somehow passed him without his noticing. Her and her smile. She opened the door wide. Ajay ignored her. He squinted into a sky gone white with clouds. The bus began rolling away. He hobbled out the door.

"Wait!" He dropped his boots. "Wait!" His voice nothing compared to the bus's rumble.

Then the Berber woman passed Ajay, his boots in her hand. She waddled after the bus, waving her crooked arms and yelling, the sound a scratch. The bus stopped. The doors opened. The Berber woman caught up and talked to the driver. She pointed to Ajay, who'd stopped to catch his breath. He looked at the ground, dizzy and hot, the air heavy with humidity. A drizzle coated Ajay's skin with a fine mist. He looked. Madina walked toward him. She stopped, making no move to help him with his bags. Her face calm as the day they first met. He smiled.

The bus driver, a paunchy man with waves of wrinkles flowing across his forehead, had one foot on the ground and the other on the first step of the bus. He yelled at Madina and Ajay to hurry up. The passengers stared out their windows, lips moving. Some laughed, others scowled.

Madina didn't look at anyone but Ajay. "Stay," she said.

"No," he said.

"Another bus—"

"No."

Ajay looked at the sky. A cool mountain breeze pushing out the heat. The air washed over his face and down his body. He closed his eyes, his thoughts tumbling, of what and when and how and why, until they slowed and stopped. He opened his eyes to Madina.

He shook his head. She kept her eyes within him. No disappointment. No judgment. No pity. She lifted his backpack and drum bag in one hand and with the other braced Ajay around the waist. He leaned against her. They walked toward the bus.

CHAPTER 13

Ajay and Madina strolled through Marrakech. Though his ankle ached and he still held a forearm against his chest to support his ribs, he felt lithe again and good, the waterfall accident nothing now but an annoyance of almost a week ago. Today the God of Luck seemed to hover close to them, which was why Ajay didn't care about the pain or the fact they were almost out of money. He walked next to long-legged Madina with the streaming black hair, and felt the closest he would ever feel to contentment. He opened his mouth to catch the wind, the air, tasting diesel fumes and dust.

They walked through streets crowded with people, the sun at their backs. There were buses and cars, modern buildings and old, a tinkling of metal and the music of birds in sudden flight. They walked beside the city wall three, maybe four stories tall where Madina stopped. Ajay walked on for several more paces before halting and turning back to Madina. She was staring up at the wall, touching the sand-colored stone with her fingers. Sweat ran down her neck.

Ajay followed her gaze to the block-like towers spaced at regular intervals along the top of the wall. A wall built centuries ago to keep out the enemy.

"They look like soldiers with pointy helmets, yes?" he said.

"Yes," Madina said and smiled at him, her eyes brilliant in the sun.

"Come," Ajay said, his smile broadening too, with the lightness he felt. "Come."

They went through the archway.

Once in the *souk*, Madina and Ajay strolled past pottery men in ragged aprons who adjusted pots tipped this way and that on their rounded bottoms. In the open center of the marketplace, a troupe of eight folk dancers jumped in their white robes and bejeweled fezzes for the tourists who stood with cameras around their necks. The crowd was lively and of good size and there was plenty of room for another performer, or two. But for now, he and Madina walked on.

They passed ropes of weaving that hung from hooks in a basket maker's shop. A donkey pulled a cart. A Muslim man rode a motorbike. Women wrapped in headscarves and colorful robes walked in twos and threes under a hot sun. Little metal awnings overhung the entrances, offering only the briefest of shade. There were bicycles, dogs, carpet dealers, grocers, trinket sellers, those selling food good enough to quell a basic hunger.

Ajay and Madina passed a boy in red shorts and a white shirt, who stood with hands on his hips, frowning at something. They passed a fortuneteller who sat at an almost-collapsed table, laying out creased cards. An old man paced back and forth yelling jokes to the crowd while a monkey sat on his shoulder shrieking *ye-ye-ye* after every punch line.

Ajay stopped before a black man who, with closed eyes, played one instrument that sounded like many. The instrument had strings, a bulbous belly and a long neck with tuning knobs on either side. The man played the strings with his thumbs while holding the neck. After awhile, the musician — his bald pate covered by a white skullcap — opened his brown eyes and smiled at Ajay, who returned the grin.

The man closed his eyes, the smile a white crescent on his face. Ajay craned his neck to peer inside the metal cup on the ground beside the man. He was good enough so that the cup should be full, but it wasn't. Too much competition. Then again, Ajay was better than any of these performers. He and Madina moved on.

Ajay was looking for something, but didn't know what, the feeling that of approaching surprise. That all a person need do was to stroll along with an open mind and eye for an opportunity that might be only steps away. So that when he saw the shop, Ajay stopped and put a hand on Madina's arm and she stopped, too. He considered the old sandals she wore.

"Sit down," Ajay said. "Take those off."

The shopkeeper sat on a mat in his stall. His long nose leaned to the left while his widely-spaced eyes pointed in opposite directions. Unsure which eye to focus on, Ajay chose the left. He pointed to brown leather sandals in a long row of pairs laid out on a dusty green carpet. The old man stood and picked up the sandals. He handed them to Ajay with a small bow.

Ajay dropped the sandals into Madina's lap. "Try them on."

Madina held the sandals in her hands, the leather almost the same color as her skin. She looked at them like she didn't know what to do. She slipped her big toe through the loop of one sandal and pulled the back strap over her heel. She put on the other sandal and stood. She lifted her skirt up to her knees, stretching one long leg and pointing her toes.

Ajay opened his mouth to make an offer, but before he could, Madina sighed. She lowered her heels and kicked off the sandals.

"What?" the shopkeeper said, palms up.

Madina sat and put on her old sandals.

"She thinks my sandals are garbage?" the shopkeeper said to Ajay.

"And she's right," Ajay said. "You charge what for these?

The man said ninety *dirham*.

"For ninety *dirham*, they should last forever," Madina said.

"They do last," the shopkeeper said. "For eighty *dirham* you will find nothing better in all the *souk*."

"Eighty?" Ajay said. "I thought you said ninety."

"Seventy-five. I said seventy-five," the shopkeeper said. "You will call me a liar next? Is that how you do business?"

"The man down the way sells his for seventy," Madina said. She stood and pointed in the direction from which they'd come.

"The man is a crook," the shopkeeper said. He stood taller. "He'll sell his for seventy, but they won't last for even that many days. But mine are strong. And for sixty-five *dirham*, they'll last for years."

"Right." Ajay turned away.

"I'll make you a deal, my final offer," the shopkeeper said. "Sixty *dirham*."

"Fifty-five," Madina said.

The shopkeeper looked at Ajay, who said nothing.

"You are robbing me, but I'll do it to prove I'm proud of my merchandise." The shopkeeper shoved the sandals at Ajay, who paid. The man threw up his hand, the one with the money in it. "You come to me next year and those sandals will look like they've never been worn. Be sure to come back so I can gloat," and he turned away.

Madina and Ajay walked past several shops before he stopped and turned to her.

"Put them on," he said.

Madina sat down on the edge of a cement trough that held a plant. She held out a hand for the sandals. Rather than drop them in her lap as he'd done before, or even hand them to her, Ajay lowered to his knees before Madina and sat back on his heels. He reached behind her left ankle and drew her foot up. With one finger he slipped off the old sandal and lowered her foot to his thigh. He removed the other sandal and placed that foot on his other thigh. Two soles against him, the pressure light, the feel warm.

Her toes were bare and thin, the bones fanning out from her ankles. The sound of voices and music floated around them. He lifted her right foot with one hand and with the other brushed the dust from her skin, first on the sides of her foot, then on the bottom. Her toes crimped and she jerked her foot, but Ajay held on. He smiled at the wiggling toes, apparently unused to being tickled. He glanced at Madina. She was smiling, just a little.

Ajay cupped her heel in his hand and slipped on the new sandal. He dressed her other foot and rested his hands on his thighs. Where her soles had been. Knees drawn to her chest, Madina looked at her feet.

"You bargain well," Ajay said.

"Thank you," Madina said.

Ajay lifted an eyebrow. "Where did you learn to do that?"

Madina told him when she was twelve or so, she heard someone grunt and curse outside her window. When she looked, she saw a man with white skin and light red hair.

"I'd never seen that color before. Almost like he'd bled and hadn't rinsed out all the blood," Madina said. She stood. They walked.

The man, Madina said, was a tourist, judging by his khakis, backpack and expensive boots. He leaned against the corner of the next house, grimacing in pain while rubbing his ankle. He looked up and stared at her with blue eyes the color of the sky when it had almost gone white with heat.

"Before I'd looked out the window, I'd drawn my scarf over my head and pulled half of it across my face and over one eye," she said. "That's what my aunt taught me to do, so I wouldn't scare anyone."

Ajay nodded. Considerate Old Aunt, who probably didn't want customers to know about the damaged goods until after they'd paid.

"The man said he was an eye doctor," Madina said, "and I thought that was strange, to have a doctor who only looked at eyes. He said when he traveled he looked for unusual eye injuries. Then he asked me what was wrong with my eye, and wanted to see it."

When Madina didn't give him an answer, the man shrugged off his backpack and took out a gold bangle. Though the circle flashed in the sun and the man set down the jewelry like it was very expensive, Madina could tell the bracelet wasn't gold. But she was used to foreigners treating her like an idiot. Ajay laughed.

"Then," and Madina stopped. She lifted her free hand like a conductor ready to start the music. "Then he pulled out a flute. The wood so pale it looked made of sand. And in every hole was pure blackness and I wondered what sound came from such darkness. I really wanted the flute." She looked at him, breathless with the memory of her desire. "But I waited, because that's what my aunt would do. She'd wait and they'd give her more. So I waited, and it was just like that." The man put two coins on the windowsill beside the bangle and flute. Madina decided that was enough. She collected the items and put them on the floor in her room.

"Then I pulled the headscarf from my face," Madina said. She arched her eyebrows, her eyes wide. "And there was nothing wrong with either one of my eyes!"

Ajay laughed.

The folk dance music ended and clapping broke out. Ajay

grabbed Madina's hands and pulled. They ran into the open space of the *souk* where the dancers had just finished. Ajay set down his green bag and took off his backpack. He and Madina had no cup or plate in which to collect their earnings, so he spread his old white and red scarf on the ground and threw a few coins onto the cloth, because no one liked to toss the first coin.

Ajay sat on the ground and set up his drums. Madina stood watching.

"Get your flute out," he said.

"My flute?"

"To play." Ajay set his second drum on the cloth donut. He drilled the drums' surfaces to warm up his hands while listening to the tone. He glanced sideways at Madina's foot, one that should have a bracelet around that slender ankle, a bracelet that was noisy and bright, to draw attention. Maybe if they made enough money today—

Madina still hadn't moved.

"Your flute!" Ajay said. "We don't have much time to capture this crowd before some bigger, noisier act comes along. If we get pushed off to the side, we won't get nearly as much money."

"You want me to play with you?"

Ajay flung his eyes at her. "You played for the man in the *casbah.*"

"I told you, I didn't mean to."

"If we play well, we'll make up the cost of those sandals and more. Enough to eat tonight."

"We have money."

"We have a little bit of money that will be gone soon." Ajay cocked his head and played a few strokes on his drum. Then he stopped, and using the small metal hammer he carried in his drum bag, adjusted the sound.

"But I only—" Madina closed her mouth.

"You only what?"

Madina blinked, the fringe of her black lashes a slow wave up and down. "I only play for—"

"For what? For pleasure? For—"

"—my Sister Wind. And you."

Ajay jumped to his feet and covered his mouth with a hand.

He paced a few times, heart moving quick, the *and you* rolling over in his mind. Ajay made his voice low and steady.

"Play for me and your Sister Wind, then," he said. "Forget everybody else."

"Play what?" she whispered.

A hot wind fingered the bottom of Ajay's T-shirt. He pointed at Madina. "Play what you told me. How the winds will destroy mankind. You never told me how they'd do it, not exactly."

Madina looked down at her pouch, her resistance wavering. Then she pulled the flute from where she slipped the instrument under the knot of her bundle.

"Begin when I say," Ajay said. "While you're at it, ask this wind to whip up a good crowd for us."

Ajay spun around. His eyes scanned the ground and stopped on a crate of chickens five steps away. He jumped on the crate and threw his arms wide, the chickens squawking. Faces turned toward the sound, toward Ajay.

"You will soon hear the best music you've ever heard in your entire life," Ajay shouted. "This music will tell you a story. Not a simple story about a broken promise or a silly quarrel, but a story that's about the end of mankind. Who among you has heard that one day the world will ignite from the sins of man? Who has heard that the sea will wash over the earth to cleanse it of lies, of hatred and greed?"

More heads turned, but not enough. Not yet.

"Death, doom, destruction!" he yelled. Now people farther out craned their necks to see who yelled. The wind grew stronger, lending credence and atmosphere to his talk of doom. He yelled louder.

"When the end of man comes, the earth will quake and the wind will unite with the oceans to pull men from their homes and into death. That means you," Ajay said and jabbed a finger at an elderly man in a white *djellabah*, the robe flapping wildly about the man's legs. "And you," Ajay said, pointing to a young man who smiled. "And you," Ajay said, indicating a foreign family of four, all of them light-skinned and light-eyed.

Ajay frowned and roamed his eyes over the crowd, an arm sweeping to include everyone. Dust blew into his eyes and made him squint. The crowd looked almost big enough. Three hundred *dirham* strong, at least.

"All of you will soon hear what will happen when the wind rises up against us," Ajay said.

A note played, then another. When he'd told her to wait. Ajay threw a hand toward Madina to signal that the truth-telling had begun, and once in motion, there would be no stopping fate. He jumped down from the crate and sat before his drums. Madina played what sounded like a prelude to hysteria, as a story of doom should. So Ajay moved into a heavy, dark beat, and to counter the gusting wind, played louder. While he would have preferred to close his eyes and concentrate on what Madina played, he squinted against the dust. Someone had to leave his eyes open to gauge the crowd and make sure no one stole from their forthcoming earnings. Soon enough, a coin flew through the air and landed on the scarf before him. He bobbed his head to the rhythm and concentrated on what Madina played.

The notes were loud and running fast already. Ajay wasn't sure how to handle the speed until he understood what she meant to do, to show people what she thought was coming, what she'd told him would happen. Of how vicious the war of winds would get, her notes representing everyone on earth. The billions of little animals that would scurry, terrified, with nowhere to run. If Madina represented humanity, Ajay would be the wind.

He recalled the image Madina painted for him on their bus journey across Morocco. If he was to play the wind, he would be *the* wind, the one that would start the war. The one he named Aaghat, the destroyer of sin.

Ajay imagined Aaghat as a broad, far-reaching wind, heavily muscled, untiring and constant. A wind that had circled high above the earth for millions of years, all the while watching and waiting. Noting how humankind treated the earth and hoping the species would change. But after a long time, Aaghat realized no good would come from the tiny, but destructive creatures. Unless Aaghat intervened, the planet would die. So when a messenger wind brought the news the opportunity had arrived to cleanse the earth, Aaghat knew it would have to strike fast, surprising the humans, or else they'd scatter and hide, a few of them surviving. A few all that was necessary for the species to thrive once again some day.

And when the day of destruction came, Ajay pictured Aaghat as a gargantuan train of strength and speed that lived so high it barreled downward for a long time before nearing the ground. Then, before unleashing its fury, it curved itself to the shape of the earth and swept close to the ground where people lived.

And when the other winds joined Aaghat, they did so with a roar and hiss, a shiver and a swoop. They funneled the anger that had built in them over the centuries as they watched a self-centered species threaten all other life forms. Thousands of winds that found any way they could to reach Aaghat. The smaller winds that caught a ride on the more powerful winds for the excitement and adventure. The wiser regional winds that grieved, but left their lands anyway, knowing they'd merge with Aaghat and cease to exist, possibly forever.

As more and more winds merged with Aaghat, the wind's strength and speed increased. Storm Pushers, Scorchers and Island Dwellers. Joker Winds, Water Winds, Ego Winds and on and on until Ajay could feel Aaghat's growing power. Could hear people screaming while trying to dig holes in which to hide and save themselves. But all such attempts were useless. A hundred, a thousand, a million times its normal strength and size, Aaghat spread out and spun around the earth until cloaking the sphere. A wind so low and fast Aaghat didn't just uproot trees or blow down buildings and whisk away cars like dust. Rather, the wind sheared all life from the earth, sweeping all animals — from elephants to the tiniest bugs and everything in between — across the land and into the oceans, and with it, their entire habitats. Their homes, nutrients, the calm necessary to mate and communicate and live. Aaghat scoured the earth, pulling great waves out of the ocean and throwing them far onto land. The wind sucked debris from deep holes and the throats of volcanoes until the earth was nothing but exposed rock and water, no soil left in which to grow plants. The wind ground down mountains to hills and hills into flatlands, the wind so constant and thorough the lucky few humans who survived — those tucked away when the attack began — starved and died. Only after all life on earth was long dead did Aaghat slow, by then the wind so heavy with dirt and debris the airborne refuse blocked the sun, bringing bitter winter for centuries to come.

Ajay's hands flew up and stopped, suspended in the air. A merciless crushing sound followed in which Ajay covered his ears and squeezed his eyes shut. He snatched a breath, then expelled the air, over and over until he could open his eyes. When he did, he saw people. They were all around him. Ajay squinted from the brightness of the daylight. He lowered his hands from his ears, the applause an explosion. Ajay's eyes leapt from face to smiling face then dropped to the scarf on the ground before him. The cloth was piled with coins, the hill growing taller every second. The mound had grown so tall some of the coins had slid off to the ground.

The sun was well past midday. He was dripping with perspiration. The wind had all but disappeared. He looked up at Madina, who stood in profile, arms at her sides, staring at her feet.

"More, more!" the crowd chanted.

Ajay jumped up, his legs cramped and ankles numb. His arms hung at his sides, weak and useless from so much playing. Yet he smiled, ready to play again, because a man could never be too rich. He opened his mouth to announce another tune, something lighter. Then he saw her face. Edged in stillness. A woman he'd forced to play her worst fear, music that brought the catastrophe out of her head and into the open, the vision that much closer to reality. The day of reckoning no longer at a distance for her, but imminent. She tried to smile. To do as he asked.

But Ajay shook his head. "The end is the end."

He squatted to gather the money, his hands shaking.

CHAPTER 14

The first man called out to Madina where she sat on the sidewalk outside a downtown Casablanca office building, waiting for Ajay to return from his errands.

The man yelled and she looked to where he stood across the four-lane street. Tall, thin and black, his smiling mouth of white teeth gleamed at the bottom of his long face. He wore jeans and a green soccer jersey and held his palm up in greeting. Madina glanced from side to side, the afternoon street crowded with pedestrians. When she looked back at him, he was still smiling at her. He waved. She stood, pouch in the crook of her left arm. She used her other hand to smooth her robe. She glanced back at the tall building behind her, then at the man. She stroked her eyebrow once, then wove her way through the people walking the sidewalk. She waited for a gap between the buses, cars and motorcycles and crossed the street. She walked to the man, who stood outside a camera shop beside a white blanket spread on the ground with various wares arranged in neat rows. Purses, wallets, sunglasses and jewelry.

"Pretty lady," he said in English accented from elsewhere. "You wait there long time. For someone *fantastique?*"

She stared at him a moment, then smiled.

"Ah, yes," and he thumped his heart with a fist. "Makhaya know about *tando.*"

Madina dropped her eyes to the blanket of wares and chewed on her smiling lip. Somewhere down the street a bell rang. Her eyes

97

wandered over the items until stopping on a short string of black beads. Black, like human eyes, and those on drums.

The street merchant picked up the beads and let them hang from his splayed fingers. "Kukui nuts. Supposed to mean peace. They protect you. Make you bright in the head, what they call… Enlighten." And he laughed.

They bargained. She paid. She stuffed the beads inside her pouch. Then another man called to her from behind. She turned.

Ajay scanned the people walking down the street in this modern business district of Casablanca. He readjusted the handle of his drum bag in his hand. Clouds had blown in overhead. He'd just lifted a substantial amount of money off a tourist in a grocer's shop, the man's carelessness seeming to insist that Ajay help himself to the four hundred *dirham* he and Madina needed for their passage to America.

Yet Ajay felt unsettled. He looked at the clouded afternoon sky, trying to guess how much two plane tickets would cost. When he'd never been on a plane. He neared the office building made of white walls and gray tinted glass. His eyes scanned the steps leading to the entrance, but Madina wasn't there. Ajay cursed. He'd left her here an hour ago and told her to wait, even though she never had before. But this time he'd hoped she would listen so he wouldn't waste time trying to find her. Because they no longer had any time to waste. They had to leave. Together. Soon.

He turned in a full circle, his eyes moving from one person to the next, all of them going nowhere and everywhere. The young woman in a beige suit and high-heels with black hair to her waist. Twin girls who crossed the street on a diagonal. A robed mother who walked with her two small children, one on either side. A man in a gray business suit.

A bell sounded. Ajay turned toward a water seller dressed in a yellow robe, green trousers and a multicolored fez. A shiny cup hung from his chest. He rang a hand bell and yelled. "Come, get a cool drink of water."

A bell, like the bells on the anklet Ajay bought for Madina after their performance in the *souk*. After fixing the anklet around her ankle, he'd smiled up at her. And she at him.

"I've belled you like a goat, so now when you wander away I can find you," he'd said.

He shivered, turning until the air blew on his face. His eyes stopped on Madina. She was sitting on the stairs in the spot where he'd left her. Gone, and now here. Gone and returned. Somewhere else and now trying to work out what she'd seen, heard and learned. And when she came to a conclusion, she'd act, which meant there was little time to save her from whatever brink she teetered on. He walked to her.

"What happened?" he asked.

"I'm not sure," she said.

"Did somebody bother you?"

"Yes. I went across the street. I bought beads for you." She held up her fist as if to give him something. He lifted his hand. She released the rope of beads slowly and they coiled there, a snake in his palm. He felt a rush of warmth in his chest. He opened his mouth. To ask if she'd stolen the necklace. But he knew she hadn't. That she wouldn't. She'd spent her own money, which made this necklace a present. His first. He slipped the beads in his pocket, unsure now of what to say or do. A present. A present for *him*. He looked into her face, so naked in its worry.

Ajay took off his backpack, set down his drum bag and squatted next to her, his back against the wall.

"Tell me," he said.

"A man came."

"What kind of man?"

"A crazy man."

"Crazy?"

"Crazier than me."

Ajay glanced at Madina, but there was no smile on her lips.

"How do you know he was crazy?" Ajay said.

"His eyes. They were light blue and red."

"Red?"

"Red veins around the blue."

"Did he ask you for money?"

Madina shook her head. "He was tall and thin. A foreigner with white skin and yellow hair. He gave me something."

Ajay rocked forward onto his feet and shifted to a squat in front of Madina.

She opened her mouth, but a moment passed before she said, "He gave me a…"

"A…a what? What did he give you?"

"An instrument."

"What kind of instrument?"

"A horn."

"Like a trumpet?"

"What's that?"

"A metal horn." Ajay held his hands apart, wider than his shoulders to indicate the length. Madina looked from one hand to the other. She shook her head.

"It's from an animal," she said.

Ajay's left eyebrow rose. Maybe she meant a tusk, which if made of ivory would be valuable. Would get them where they needed to go.

"Where is it?" Ajay said

"I threw it away."

Ajay smacked his hand on his thigh. "Why did you do that?"

Madina looked away, but Ajay caught her wrist and forced her to look at him.

"Because," Madina said, "it could end the world."

It could end the world; her answer to everything she found disturbing. He rested his forearms on his thighs.

"I don't understand," he said.

"A man was running down the street. He saw me and ran over."

"What did he look like?"

"Blue eyes—"

"No. How did he act."

Madina looked at the ground. "He was sweating. His shirt was untucked. He seemed like he was telling the truth and that the truth was both secret and at the same time funny."

"Then what?"

"Then he gave me the horn. He told me one blow would call forth the end of mankind. Then he smiled."

Ajay shot to a stand. He paced back and forth and rubbed a

100

hand along his jawbone. He reached down and with one hand scooped up his backpack and drum bag. With the other he grabbed Madina under her arm and hauled her up, making her scramble to grasp her pouch. He led her down the street and pulled her into an alley. He spun her around and pushed her to the wall, pinning her against it.

"I don't understand you, Madina," Ajay said. He moved his eyes from one green orb to the other and back.

"You have this crazy thing about winds, yet you know it's crazy," Ajay said. "You believe evil winds are trying to kill all mankind and now, today, you just happen to be handed the very instrument that will start the destruction. But instead of keeping it, you throw it away! Well I don't see the man, Madina, and I don't see this—" and he threw his hand so close to Madina's face she flinched. "—this animal horn. Which is very convenient, don't you think? To have nothing to prove or *disprove* your story? Well I've had enough. You can't be crazy anymore. I forbid it!"

Ajay released her and paced two steps and turned. The beads she gave him. The anklet he gave her. The way she'd pawed at the earth to find water in the desert. How she'd looked wearing his T-shirt. The way she held his mirror while he trimmed his mustache. The melding of their music in the market, and not for the crowd, either, but for each other, for *him*. All that, yet now she seemed to cast all those moments into the winds that held her in their grip, reverting to her firm belief in the reality of the winds he was trying to excise from her mind.

"Come, get a cool drink of water," the water seller cried, his bells ringing.

Ajay glared at Madina, chest heaving. Madina's face had hardened into stone, so that now he'd have to crack her open again. And again and again.

"All right," Ajay said. "If you threw this horn away, where is it? I want it in my hand."

When Madina didn't move, Ajay sniffed. So he was right. There was no horn. But then Madina turned and with two strides was back on the sidewalk, moving away. Ajay gripped his bags and followed.

They walked back the way they came, past the white office

building to a sidewalk café. She led him to a garbage can camouflaged from customers by a potted plant the size of a rotund man. Ajay peered into the lidless can half-filled with food scraps. Soggy bread, wilted lettuce, chicken bones, parsley, melon rinds, tea leaves.

Ajay surveyed the area, including the diners and pedestrians walking by. He peered through the screen door into the café's kitchen. If only the water seller would shut up and stop ringing those bells. Ajay leaned over the can and reached a hand into the garbage. Into the squish of liquid and leftover food.

He groped from side to side, going deeper with each sweep. But he felt nothing. He shook his head and exhaled. Then his fingers touched something hard. Something wider than a chicken bone and less craggy than a lamb bone. Ajay walked his fingertips up the curved object, which wasn't much longer than his hand. He got a grip and pulled. He stared at the foreigner's gift to Madina. The object was a horn rather than a tusk. Hollow and worthless instead of valuable. Of honey hue, the horn's broad, open end spiraled down to a pointed tip with a small hole. Coffee grinds and vegetable cuttings clung to the rough surface.

A waiter came out the kitchen door. Ajay moved away from the can and Madina stepped in front of him. The waiter glanced at her and passed. Ajay stood and stepped back from Madina. He'd demanded proof and she'd produced an object to fit her story. Maybe someone had given her the horn, and maybe not.

Ajay glanced both ways and reached toward a cart holding a bin of dirty dishes. He lifted a pitcher from the bin and poured water over the horn and over his hand. Though cleaner, the thing was still a small, worthless animal part. He lodged the item under his arm and picked up his backpack in one hand and drum bag in the other. He guided Madina back to the alley and put down his things in order to study the instrument closer. He lifted the pointed end to his eye, squinted and peered through the small hole. Though conceivably blowing through the hole would produce a sound, the result couldn't amount to more than a toot, much less than a series of vibrations that would signal the end of the world. Ajay lifted the instrument to his lips, ready to blow.

He saw her arm, but only when there was no time left to protect himself. When Madina slapped the instrument, the tip dug into the roof of his mouth. He sucked in air with a hiss through clenched teeth and lunged toward Madina, who jumped back, shoulders hunching around her ears and hands coming up to fend him off. He gripped the horn with his fist and tongued the gouge in his mouth.

"What's the matter with you?" he said.

"Don't blow it," she said. Tone harsh. Eyes brutal.

"It's an instrument," Ajay said. "Instruments are for playing."

"Not ones that call down destruction."

"This one is so puny it couldn't call a cat to dinner if the cat were starving and right under foot."

They glared at one another, Madina's eyes fiercer than he'd ever seen them. The warrior returned. He laughed, a surprise even to him. Once begun, the reaction escalated beyond his control. Not that he wanted to stop. He'd laugh for however long was necessary to gain a purchase amid such ridiculousness.

Ajay held his ribs and leaned over, a hand on his knee. When the laughing subsided, he wiped his eyes and leaned back against the wall. The roof of his mouth ached.

"No wonder the man looked like he wanted to laugh, considering how willingly you swallowed his story," Ajay said. He slid down the wall until he sat on his haunches. He stared at the instrument and shook his head.

"You really think this thing is going to call down Aaghat, don't you?" Ajay said.

"Aaghat?"

"The big wind high up. The one waiting for the signal to come down and wipe everybody off the earth."

Madina remained silent. Ajay motioned for her to sit. She squatted, but out of arm's reach.

"I think you were right in at least one thing, Madina, the man who handed you the horn was crazy. But not crazier than you are, to believe what he told you."

Madina's eyes dropped to the horn in Ajay's hand.

"Look at this thing," Ajay said. He twisted the horn one way, then the other. "It's a small horn an animal shed. If I were to blow it, it would probably just squeak. How could a squeak make its way up to a wind many kilometers above the earth?"

"But what if it can?"

"It can't."

"You don't know that. Winds can carry sound—"

"Not that far."

"You don't know."

Ajay jumped to his feet, arms flying out to either side of him.

"I know that you're living in a fantasy world where you're the center of attention. A world you made up because out here," and Ajay jabbed a fist toward the sidewalk and the people passing and the noise of living, "you're not important at all. None of us is."

Madina pinched her lips closed. Ajay's eyes rose up the canyon between the buildings to the white sky above. The wind damp. The alley smelling of oil and garbage. He sighed. He was tired now, too tired to disprove her anymore. He wished he hadn't said she wasn't important. Though true when considering humanity as a whole and beyond that, the size of the universe, the statement was also untrue. While one person's actions meant nothing when lumped with everyone else's — for days, years, decades, centuries — a single deed at the right moment could mean everything. The difference between life and death, destruction and salvation. Ajay shook his head. At how she trembled. At how her eyes bounced between the horn and his face. The expression of someone gripping a miniscule ledge of rock, a thousand-meter fall just moments away. Someone who now cared if she lived or died.

Ajay massaged the roof of his mouth with his tongue. "You think the evil winds will try to get you to blow this horn and end mankind, yes?"

Madina swallowed and looked at the ground.

Ajay used the tip of the horn to scratch his forehead. "Well, what should we do with it?"

"Throw it away," Madina said.

"Someone might fish it out like I did and blow it."

Madina stroked her eyebrow several times. "What do you think, then?"

"What do *I* think?"

When she'd never asked his opinion before.

"Well," he said, "if it makes you feel better, you could throw it in the ocean. That way no one would ever get hold of it." Then he smiled. "You've never seen the ocean, have you?"

Madina shook her head.

"Well you will," he said. "More ocean than you could ever want. Because that's what I wanted to tell you, I just bought passage for us on a ship to America. When we're far out to sea, you can throw this overboard." He lifted the horn, his palm open. Offering Madina the instrument. But instead she stepped back and spread her arms flat against the alley wall, her eyes wide.

"Then I'll do it for you," Ajay said.

"I want to see. When you throw it into the ocean," she said. "I want to see that."

"That'll make you feel better?" Ajay said.

"Yes."

"All right," Ajay said. He pushed the horn to the bottom of his backpack. Yet when he hoisted the pack, the tip poked him in the lower back. He jiggled the pack until he didn't feel the point anymore.

"Come," he said. "I'm hungry. Let's get something to eat." He took her elbow and led her out of the alley. He smiled "Tomorrow I have to do a few last errands. Then we'll disappear from this place."

They would leave and he would continue to lead her farther and farther away from her lunacy, to the consummation of the resolve formed by Ajay in the desert beside the burning tree. He would dig and probe for proof Madina didn't have to carry the world on her shoulders. That she wasn't responsible for mankind's downfall. Then, when the right moment came, he'd hand her the evidence in a way she'd have to accept. At first she'd stare at her feet. Then she would swallow and blink and lift her eyes and for the first time, the voices in her head would disappear and the wind would simply be the wind. Stunned by the quiet, the calm, she'd inhale. She'd look around, and when she did, she'd see Ajay. Finally. Then life would be good.

CHAPTER 15

Ajay sat on the sand, eyes on the morning ocean, a dark gray that melded with the clouds above. He hugged his arms around his knees, his sweater not enough protection against the sea wind that had blown all night and continued to drive full into his face. The sea birds banked and dove toward the sand, picking at bits of food buried there, leftovers from tourists. When one bird found a treasure, others came, all screeching and fighting until one flew off with the morsel. Otherwise the beach was empty.

Madina lay on her side in the sand, her back to him and head resting on her outstretched arm. His eyes moved from her hair down the scoop of her neck, up and over the slope of her shoulder to her arm, the elbow lodged in the valley of her waist. From there her hip rose, a mountain that tapered to the legs, a long, gentle descent that ended at her bare feet. What would fitting oneself to such a body feel like? The round of her behind against one's crotch. The warmth of the skin against one's chest, a hand resting in the curve of that waist. Ajay returned his gaze to the ocean and fingered the black bead necklace he wore around his throat.

A freighter passed so far away the ship seemed a dark shadow, one moving away. He and Madina would be on a similar ship in less than twenty-four hours. He was late in reaching his destination, but at least they'd get there. And if his opportunity had passed, Madina would be there, creating a new chance. As long as he

107

was there, she would be all right and he would know she was safe and not have to guess about whether she'd lived or died. He shivered and rubbed his arms. If only she hadn't seen the ocean.

They'd gotten to the beach last night, the sky filled with the burn of sunset. Madina's eyes bypassed the crimson-purple-orange conflagration and went straight to the ocean. Mouth open, she swept her eyes right and left, evidently unable to fathom the vastness of what lay before her. At the same time she seemed to open herself even more, allowing the sea to pour in. How much could a normal person take before being overwhelmed? Then again, Madina wasn't usual. Rather than becoming humbled before the sight, she seemed to expand and grow stronger. To sit straighter, taller, electricity arcing from her fingertips even when she rested.

Ajay had wanted to sleep somewhere else — somewhere less open to thieves or the police — but Madina had ignored him, though that word wasn't quite right. She seemed unable to hear him. She sat in the sand, staring, as the light turned her face to wine and her eyes to glass.

Before the last of daylight vanished, Ajay had asked Madina if she wanted him to get rid of the horn here and now. To throw the instrument far out, the deed done, with no more need to worry. But she said no. If they didn't throw the instrument far enough, it might wash back onto the beach. They would do what Ajay suggested and bury the horn deep in the sea. Now that she'd seen the ocean, she seemed convinced of its capacity to hide the instrument forever.

Ajay stood and shivered. He stretched, wiggled his toes and stuck his hands under his armpits, then walked around Madina and sank on his knees before her. She was sleeping, which was good, last night one of the first in a long while she hadn't been plagued by nightmares. Those whimperings of irregular breath, quick and partial. Of only moments left to live. He leaned forward and peered into her face, so relaxed, her lashes long and the scar pale in the gray light.

Madina opened her eyes, the movement so sudden Ajay fell back on his behind.

"*Yadda!*" he said. "I thought you were asleep."

"I haven't been asleep all night."

"Not at all?"

"No."

108

"That's too bad."

Madina rolled to her back and stared at the sky, the clouds reflecting in her eyes.

"That's not bad, that's good," she said. "I've been listening to the water and wind all night."

Ajay turned himself to face the ocean. "You listen to the water now, too?"

Madina sat up beside him. She watched the water with half-closed eyes.

"At first I thought this water was an animal that moves and breathes," Madina said. "An animal possessing a tremendous body. Then I thought maybe it was just a big thing the wind moved by pushing along its surface. Shoving waves toward shore. Now I think the wind and water are both animals. One tethered to the sky, the other to the earth."

Madina lifted her nose and inhaled, her expression one of smelling perfume. "Do you feel how long and flat the Ocean Wind stretches? How tired it is, traveling for so long without anything to slow it down or provide it with companionship? A solitary wind of duty. It possesses no malice. None. If not gentle, at least this wind feels honest."

Small waves broke on the shore.

"The story," she said. "Tell me the rest of the story."

Ajay looked away. He used his right hand to spread the sand flat beside him, the smell of saltwater and sea decay sharp in his nose.

"What story?" he said.

"The one about the husband and wife. He was swallowed by a fish and she was so sad her relatives took her to a doctor."

"She got better."

Seagulls landed close to Ajay. He threw a pebble at them and they flew off, yelling at one another. Ajay used his finger to smooth his mustache. But still Madina waited.

"The relatives told the doctor, 'Please help this old woman overcome her grief.' The doctor asked the old woman whether she had loved her husband. She said she would love him forever, whether he was alive or dead. Then the doctor gave her a mysterious powder to take each day for seven days."

"What kind of powder was it?"

"I just told you, a *mysterious* powder. Anyway, the old woman did as she was told and by the end of the seventh day had quit her crying and shrieking and tearing of hair and once again began to live a quiet life. The end."

"Was the powder magical?" Madina said in English.

Ajay flicked his hand from the wrist. "I don't know," he said in Arabic. "She was cured. That's all I can remember."

He got to his feet. "Come on. Let's get something to eat, then I have some business to do and with any luck we'll be on our way to America." He turned his back on the ocean and looked up the beach and toward the skyward luxury hotels and restaurants and expensive clothing stores. He told himself he shouldn't look at her, and wouldn't.

But then Madina rose. She stood tall before him, blocking his view of the buildings of white, green and copper. If he looked at her now, he'd tell the rest of the story and be sorry. So he lowered his eyes and walked around her. He picked up his things and headed up the beach.

The air was warm and the sun a white disc through thin cloud cover. The wind had softened to a breeze. Madina and Ajay walked down streets made for rich tourists, the stores of clean glass and few items, of dim lighting and single flowers in vases set atop pedestals.

Madina peered into every store they passed. She turned around to watch people walk down the street, clean bags in hand. Her open mouth, the intensity of her gaze returned. Not just looking at anything, but again looking for something in particular. That next clue of where to go and what to do. Wherever she looked, he looked, his right hand drumming against his thigh.

Madina stopped and looked in a jewelry shop window. Ajay squinted at the sparkling gems in their gold and silver settings, some of the stones so big they could fill one's fist. Red reds and blue blues and the cleanest of whites. Any single one of them could pay for two first-class tickets on the cruise ships Ajay had seen slipping along the Mediterranean. The kind of vessel that had swimming pools, deck chairs and long tables of food.

He followed Madina's gaze through the window into the shop. To a slim man, a foreigner with brown hair, prominent forehead and thin lips. He wore beige slacks and a white shirt and his hand rested on the hip of a small brunette woman standing next to him. While the woman studied the jewelry the man studied Madina, a mixture of fascination, disdain and want in his brown eyes.

Madina turned and walked down the street. As though she hadn't seen the man staring at her or how he'd done so. A woman who once walked with stooped shoulders and downcast eyes, the pouch clutched tight against her ribs. Whereas now she moved within a flowering skirt amidst the music of bells, one hand gripping her pouch, arms swinging, strides so long she was leaving him behind. When they were almost there, almost safe.

Ajay stopped. Madina walked on. Then she stopped and looked up, apparently startled. She looked around. She turned to him.

"What's wrong?" she said.

A white limousine crossed the sidewalk in front of Madina and Ajay and pulled into the circular driveway of a hotel with delicate balconies leafing off the tall white walls. When he and Madina neared the entrance of wide gold doors, Ajay caught a glimpse of palm trees inside.

"Come," he said.

They walked up the white marble steps to the doors, which a doorman opened. Madina and Ajay walked in and stood in the lobby on a carpet of dark green with an intricate design of gold, rose and blue. Madina tilted her head back, eyes on the ceiling three stories above, one painted to mimic the sky with all its light and life, but none of its movement. Two sets of curved marble stairs led to a mezzanine while to the left, a wall of palm fronds shielded a bar.

Ajay led the way around the tall greens that waved in the air conditioned breeze. They entered the lounge and passed a number of empty glass tables on their way to the dark wood bar where an Asian man sat talking to the woman bartender, an older woman with high cheekbones, a pile of dark hair and half-closed eyes. She greeted Ajay and Madina with what looked like a permanent smile that neither increased nor diminished. Yet her eyes lingered on Madina.

"*Bonjour*," the bartender said.

111

Ajay cleared his throat, trying to remember the French word for *water*.

Before he could say anything, Madina said, *"Bonjour. Nous voudrions de l'eau, s'il vous plait."*

Ajay smiled and nodded, hiding his shock. Madina had told him she knew a little French. But fluency was not quite the same thing as *a little*. Just as disturbing was the royal tone of her voice in asking for water. This desert queen, just arrived from her oasis palace. What other surprises and secrets did Madina have locked in her heart?

The bartender put two glasses of ice water on the bar, each on a square of white napkin. She nodded at Madina with the same smile. The Asian man rattled his glass of ice. Ajay took their drinks and led Madina to a table in the far corner near a white baby grand piano. They sat and drank.

"I need to go out," Ajay said. "There are a few things I have to do before we leave. This is the third time I'm asking you, telling you, don't—"

Madina's eyes swung to the ceiling and she cocked an ear. Ajay rapped on the table with his knuckles. Madina blinked and looked at him. No idea, apparently, of what he'd just said.

"Don't keep me in suspense," Ajay said. "What important message has the wind come to impart this time? The address of where this war will take place? A specific time, perhaps?"

Madina lowered her eyes to the table and rolled her lips together, queenly one moment and meek the next.

"Are you sure you don't have anything to share?" He waited, but she said nothing. "As I was saying. Please. I'm begging you. Stay here, yes?"

She still wouldn't look at him, but nodded. Ajay lifted his glass to his lips and filled his cheeks with ice. He rose, put on his backpack and picked up his drum bag.

"Please," he said.

Madina nodded.

"Would you rather come with me?"

She considered him, then shook her head.

"All right, then." He walked out.

112

Madina watched him go. She rose and walked to the bar, her pouch tucked into the crook of her arm.

"Another, please," she said in French.

The bartender filled the glass. Madina drank to the bottom.

"You on vacation?" the Asian man said in English.

Madina set down the glass and looked at the man, who sat two barstools away. He wore blue trousers, a red shirt and wire-rimmed glasses. His teeth almost too white against his olive skin.

"I am," he said and swiveled to face her. He leaned an elbow on the bar and used one hand to stir his drink.

The bartender refilled Madina's glass with water.

"*Merci*," Madina murmured. The bartender nodded and moved away, the dim smile ever present. So cool. So knowing.

The man leaned toward her and almost yelled. "Do you speak English?"

Madina considered the man. She nodded.

"Thank god," and the man leaned back, smiling. "Anyway, I'm on vacation. To escape the weather." His eyes flew wide. "I'm sorry, I forgot my manners. Have a seat." He smiled and gestured at the barstool next to his.

Madina hesitated, then sat on the nearest barstool, which left a vacant seat between them. The man's smile grew bigger. He held out his hand to shake.

"Dave Chin, insurance adjuster for Coast to Coast Insurance in Indianapolis, Indiana. That's in America," he said.

Madina looked at his hand. She extended her own. They shook, he more vigorously than she. Dave dropped her hand.

"And your name is…?" he said, leaning forward.

Madina paused. He waited. She told him.

"Well how the hell are you, Madina?" he said, his head nodding and knee bouncing. When she didn't say anything, he said. "That's right. I needed a vacation because — being in insurance and all — I have to deal with disasters and there are too the fuck many of them lately, if you'll pardon my French. Last few years? Woohoo. It's like things have been going crazy. We had a tornado in Salt Lake City, for god's sake. Salt Lake City never has tornadoes. What's next? Snow in Miami?" He shook his head and drank from his glass.

"What's *tornadoes*?" Madina said.

His eyes widened. "You've never seen a tornado?"

Madina shook her head.

"That's lucky." Dave wiped a hand down the side of his smooth jaw. "It's a big cone of swirling wind." He pointed a finger at the ceiling and twirled while moving his arm up, up, up.

Madina pointed at his hand. "Whirlwinds," she said, whirling her finger upward, too.

"No, no," Dave said. "Whirlwinds are nothing. Tornadoes are big suckers," and he raised both arms high in the air. "Bigger than tall buildings. Nastiest things you ever want to see."

Madina frowned.

"All smelly and green, blasting away like a jackhammer wherever it touches," Dave said. "Think of a big bulldozer coming down from the clouds." He lowered his hand, fingers curling toward the floor. "And this bulldozer just crushes the hell out of anything in its path."

"They kill people?"

"Oh, yeah," the man said. He leaned back and put his hand on his thigh again. "Especially if you live in a mobile home park." He laughed, his shoulders jumping.

"Do they have tornadoes in Montana?" Madina asked.

The man considered. "Now there's a place I haven't been yet. Maybe. But Illinois or Oklahoma or Kansas are your best bet."

Dave swung around to the bar, finished his drink and ordered another. He leaned his elbows on the counter and glanced at Madina, his eyes slipping down her body before coming back to her face.

"You'll have to pardon me," Dave said. "I think I'm overworked. Like I said, this is a vacation for me. My sister works for the airline and gets free tickets, so two nights ago, I'm thinking to myself, Dave, you've got to get out of town. You've just spent three weeks in thigh-high boots because New Jersey flooded. When only the year before they'd had a bitch of a drought, if you can imagine that. And before that it was an earthquake in southern California and before that, flooding of the Mississippi and get *this*, wildfires in Pennsylvania. Pennsylvania!" He shook his head. "Fires, electrical storms, floods. And every year it seems to get worse, and I've been in the business for fifteen years. Jesus, how many disasters can a guy take? So I tell my sister, I got to get out of here before hurricane

114

season starts. Leaving during hurricane season is like being an accountant who goes on vacation during tax season. Of course my boss gave me shit, and I was ready to tell her, Why don't you go wear thigh-high boots for three weeks and talk to those sobbing people who have to float by their homes in boats? Miraculously, she caught on to the fact I was kind of on edge and maybe I needed to get away. So I asked my sister, Where can I go? And she said, Morocco. I said, Do they have tornadoes or hurricanes or flooding there? I don't think so, she said, and I'm like, That's where I'm going."

"Hurricanes?" Madina said.

Dave laughed. When her expression didn't change, he stopped laughing.

"You don't know about hurricanes, either?" he said.

"I come from the desert," she said.

"The desert. Jesus. Well I guess you wouldn't, would you? A hurricane is a big, huge storm that develops over the sea. Then it runs into land and sends people's brand new Mercedes crashing into brick walls." He leaned toward her and lowered his voice. "Thank god I don't have a Mercedes." He laughed. Then his smile vanished. He stared at Madina. He leaned forward again, one elbow on the bar. He lowered his voice. "See, I've got this theory. Nuclear attacks? Meteors striking earth? Deadly viruses? Uh-uh. Mother Nature is going to get us."

"Mother Nature?" Madina said.

"The weather." Dave dipped his head up and down several times. "Record-setting rains, record-setting heat, record-setting droughts." He slapped the counter with his palm.

"The wind," Madina said.

"What about the wind?"

"The weather, the wind... It's a problem?"

"Oh, hell yes! Wind is always a problem," Dave said. "Man, I hate wind. Tornadoes, hurricanes, tsunamis. The stuff I've seen. Houses wiped clean off their foundations like food off a plate. Telephone poles wrapped around trees. Hundred-foot yachts that start out in the harbor and get driven through the front windows of department stores two blocks away.

"Do you know how fast hurricane winds can go?" Dave didn't wait for a reply. "One hundred and fifty miles per hour,

115

sometimes faster. Can you imagine that? I can't imagine that and I've been around after hurricanes have died down. It's all you can do to stand up straight."

Dave shook his head. "I'm telling you," he said and thumbed the side of his nose a few times. "Mother Nature, she's retaliating. And let me tell you, she's one tough bi— lady." Dave dropped his eyes to his drink, still shaking his head. When he looked up, he smiled.

"But what good does it do to be depressed. Live for the moment." He hoisted his glass and swallowed. Then he looked at Madina. He drew his finger down his cheek, from eye to mouth, then pointed to Madina's scar. "Do you mind if I ask what happened?"

Madina remained silent.

Dave lifted a palm to her. "No problemo. That's what I get for being nosy. Listen," and he lowered his voice and leaned forward. "You want to come up to my room? We could forget about the world for awhile, as the song goes."

Madina didn't move.

"My room is really nice," Dave said, smiling. He hopped off his seat and stood with a hand out, showing the way.

Madina turned her head to look at the bartender. Though she lowered her eyes, the smile remained. As if she knew what Madina would do. Madina swiveled around on her barstool and stood before Dave, who was only a little taller. Together they walked up the waterfall of white stairs and along the hallway to a door. Dave opened the door and walked in.

The wide room was decorated in gold and blue and had an almost black wood desk and matching chairs. The dark contrasted with the white of the walls and carpet, making the room appear dim and cool. The ocean of heavy blue drapes swooped on either side of the wide glass sliding doors that led to a slim porch with pots of swaying palms. A beam of wan afternoon sunlight lay across the floor. And at the center of the room was a large bed covered in a material that seemed to glimmer and shift in the light, like water.

"Come on in," he said. He smiled, took off his glasses and set them on the desk, a small click in the quiet.

Madina continued to stand in the hall outside the door. She stared at the bed. Her gaze shifted to Dave, who walked toward her, a hand out. Madina took a step back. Dave stopped. They stood, one in the dim hall, the other in a room of gold and blue, the light thin. Madina turned and walked down the hall.

"Where you going?" Dave said.

She went down the stairs, past the restaurant and out the gold doors.

The man laughed and set a pile of bills on the table before Ajay. The two sat on cushions at a low table in the back room of the man's rug store. Out front the man sold wool flat-weave rugs of orange, scarlet and dark blue, while back here he exchanged money on the black market. The man had been fair and Ajay felt good. Less than twelve hours from boarding the freighter, he now had a stack of American dollars, enough to get them to New York. Enough, yet Ajay's eyes slid from his small stack of bills to the man's large pile.

"Now that business is over, perhaps you'll tell me where I can find a good pigeon pie," Ajay said. He smiled at the man, who looked like a thumb, what with his bald head, flat face and plug-like body.

The man nodded and smiled, his two front teeth protruding beyond his lower lip. "Of course, of course. As a Moroccan welcoming a stranger, I can, with confidence, recommend a place not far from here. A place owned by my brother's father-in-law. Not only is the pigeon pie delicious, but their *b'stilla* is flaky and the *brochette de kabob*..." The man smiled and shook his head. Then he raised one finger. "Do you know what it is, friend, that makes a superb pigeon pie?"

"If someone else pays for it," Ajay said.

The man leaned back and laughed. Ajay smiled. The man nodded and set a hand atop his mound of dollars.

"Yes, that would make any pigeon pie taste better. Not the answer I was looking for, of course, but a better one, without a doubt. Now, would you care for a cup of tea to conclude our negotiations?"

"Yes, thank you," Ajay said.

The man got to his feet, walked to a cart along the concrete wall and turned his back to prepare the tea. Ajay glanced at the man's stack of bills only a reach away. With a few more dollars, Ajay could get a hotel room for Madina. A room in a fancy hotel of white walls and polished furniture, the carpet soft under her feet. She could feel the silkiness of luxury for once. Then he and she would eat and drink whatever they wanted and for the first time not feel half-starved.

Though Ajay heard a thin stream of water pouring into a cup, the sound seemed far away, insignificant, at least compared to the image of Madina stretched out on a beautiful bed in a beautiful room, a shiver of sheets on her gold skin. From that sea of softness, she'd look up at him and smile, then lift a hand toward him and he'd reach for her—

The back of Ajay's hand seemed to catch fire. He snatched his hand to his chest, hissing with pain from the burn of boiling water. He rocked back and forth, catching a glimpse of the man, who stood beside the table with an empty cup in hand. Tea covered the table, soaking Ajay's stack of bills and running off the edge onto his pants. When he caught his breath, he blew on his hand, which was already red.

The man pulled two dry bills from the middle of Ajay's pile and put them back on his own stack.

"Consider this *bakshish*, for my professional services," the man said. Then he took two more bills from Ajay. "And this. Well, let's just say your crude behavior will pay for my pigeon pie tonight, my friend."

The room had no window, yet a breeze crawled across Ajay's neck.

Ajay walked with his chin down, his burned hand raised to reduce the throbbing. He gripped his drum bag with his left hand and strode through the business district toward the hotel where he left her. This time she'd better be there.

"Madina," Ajay whispered through gritted teeth. If he'd separated from her long ago, he would never have lost himself in daydreaming and gotten his hand burned, the one he needed to earn his living and live his art. Without her, he would have concentrated and moved so fast the man would never have known of the small theft.

Birds flew up between the office buildings. Gray clouds rolled low overhead. The air smelled of exhaust and mint and damp concrete. Cars passed. People hurried, held hands and called to one another. They left buildings and entered.

Caught. When he *never* got caught, his ability to get in and out fast his second greatest talent behind that of his drum playing. Without his swiftness, he would never have survived this long. Was he now losing that advantage? Slowing down to the point where he'd gotten caught and punished. What would happen next time?

Madina like a dust storm in his mind, her particles whirling around, confusing him, dulling his senses and obscuring his view. She was suffocating him. Yet, unlike a desert storm that would eventually die down, she only got stronger in his mind. He choked on the images of her body close to his when really she always seemed kilometers away. In another country. Another universe. A person so far away and yet able to cause so much trouble.

Ajay shivered in the strong ocean wind blowing against him. Always the stupid winds! Workers and whisperers and sisters and land lovers. He turned his head and caught his image in the mirrored window of a bank, the vision a mixture of light, glass and shadow flying by.

The hotel came into view. Ajay pressed his shoulders back and plunged on. He turned in at the circular driveway, ran up the stairs and flung open the door before the doorman could. Ajay swung left around the wall of palms to the bar. He looked around. Empty. Of course. How stupid to assume she'd actually be where he had told her to stay. The bartender looked up from her magazine, the same smile, so smug. Like she'd known all along Madina would leave him.

Well this time he was unwilling to wait. To search. He'd be on that freighter with or without Madina. He walked back through the lobby and extended an arm to open the door, but the doorman responded first. Ajay kept his eyes on the ground and jogged down the steps.

"Ajay."

Ajay stopped and turned. Madina stood off to the right on the top step. One arm hung at her side and the other clutched her pouch. She was looking at him with a peculiar intensity, unlike her characteristic far-away expression.

Ajay's heart boomed with the collision of his anger at her hold on him and his desire for her. Because if he gave in to the latter

— if he lost his ability to think quickly — he could die. His burned hand a case in point.

"That's the first time you've said my name," he said. "All this time — in the desert, almost dying, in the *souk* — and this is the first time you manage to make yourself say it?"

Madina opened her mouth, but said nothing. A strand of black hair blew across her cheek and caught under her chin.

Ajay ran up the steps, grabbed Madina's upper arm and led her down the sidewalk past the tourists and cars and buses and shops and apartment buildings. He dragged her through a tangle of smells on the wind, of exhaust, perfume, cinnamon and ocean. He pulled her across a busy street to a small park with palm trees and concrete benches where he sat down, pulling Madina down beside him. Madina's eyes spotted his hand. She pointed, her mouth open.

"Forget it," he snapped, and put his hand behind his back. The wind grew stronger. "Let me finish telling you the story of the woman whose husband died," he said, "the truth. Her husband died and she swallowed the powder to relieve her grief and it worked. Well there happened to be a boy in the village — one of the old woman's many irritatingly curious grandsons — and he wanted to know for sure if the powder was magical. So he went to the old doctor and asked him." Ajay stopped and looked away from Madina. He couldn't see her with his eyes, but he could see her in his mind. The way the wind made her hair fly in all directions.

"Well, the old doctor just shrugged," Ajay said, "and asked the boy, 'If you get up every morning and do the same thing at the same time, what's that called?'

'A habit,' the boy said.

'Yes,' the old man said." Ajay turned his head to face Madina. "Do you know what he meant, Madina? That love is a habit. All this talk of everlasting bliss, it's all just a habit. One gets used to somebody and it's better to be with that person than alone. So used to that person there's nothing left to discover. That person acts, you react, until a pattern forms. That person does this," and Ajay sliced a hand to the right, "and you do that. The girl meets the boy and they get used to one another. The powder wasn't magical, do you understand? All it did was make the woman wait until her habit — her reliance on her husband — was broken."

The horn of a scooter beeped while passing. Ajay swiveled his head and caught the image of a woman in jeans and white shirt, moving away fast. Ajay looked to the sky. The clouds had descended lower and the wind increased in strength and coolness. He brought his eyes back to Madina and found her looking at him, her eyes calm, as he knew they would be. He didn't look away.

A raindrop splashed the bridge of Ajay's nose and slid into the corner of his eye, then down his cheek. A second drop hit his forehead. He laughed, his teeth clenched. Rain, exactly what he needed to douse the burn. The rain descended, an ocean closing over, submerging them both. Ajay linked his arm through Madina's and made her run.

CHAPTER 16

Ajay pulled Madina through the open front of a small food market and stopped. He dropped her arm, turned, and panted, watching the rain pour. The gusting wind made the water skate sideways. Ajay shook the water from his drum bag. His burned hand felt doubled in size, but the cold rain had soothed the pain a bit. He used the hand to point outside.

"What kind of wind is that and what's it saying?" Ajay asked Madina. "Come on now, don't be shy."

Madina said nothing.

Ajay shrugged his shoulders and backpack, rain pooling around his feet. How funny, wanting to avoid what he had most desired in the desert. How he would have loved this downpour then. The contents of the pack shifted and the mouthpiece of the horn poked him in the back. Ajay shimmied his upper body again, but the tip of the horn bored into him, low and deep. He took off the backpack and walked up the aisle, scanning the overpriced goods. These fancy packages of fruit, tea and candy. The cans of marinades and sauces, of disposable cameras and postcards and CDs of *authentic* Moroccan music. The store was empty. No one even stood behind the counter to guard the register.

"You waited too long to get out of the rain," a man said in Arabic.

A bearded, middle-aged man walked out from behind the curtained doorway of a back room and sat on a stool. He had a large

123

lump on his forehead over his left eye. The man smiled and set his elbow on the register. With the other hand, he waved Ajay in.

"Come, come," he said. "I have no one. You are my only customer…" The man's eyes drifted over Ajay's shoulder. The man's eyebrows lifted and his smile grew wider.

Ajay glanced over his shoulder to see Madina walking up the aisle, her water-weighted hair longer than usual. Her wet clothes outlined her body and raindrops slid down her arms.

The man clapped his hands, hopped off his stool and disappeared through the curtained doorway. He came back with three small glasses of steaming gold liquid.

"Here," the man said. "Some tea for us. Very fine, from India."

Tea. How ironic. But Ajay was hungry and thirsty. He walked to the counter, close enough to see the shopkeeper's graying chest hairs where his blue shirt opened at the neck. Ajay set down his belongings and accepted the tea with his uninjured hand. He inhaled the mint scent.

"It's very hot, so be careful," the man said and blew on his tea before taking a small sip.

Ajay placed his lower lip on the cup's edge and exhaled, the steam warming his nose. She had asked him. He'd been obliged to tell. Just as he was obliged to take her to New York as he said he would. Feeling strong, sharp. Ready and willing to thwart any last stunt she pulled. Then his obligation — his first and last — would end.

"You're just visiting Morocco, is that right?" the man said and sat on his stool again, glass in hand.

Ajay said yes.

The shopkeeper looked at Madina, eyes moving from her face to her waist. Then he shifted his eyes to Ajay and smiled the kind of smile a man gives another man when approving his choice of female.

Ajay looked away and sipped his tea. "This is my wife."

The man's eyebrows shot up. "Ah, I see. And here I thought you were brother and sister." The man smiled at Ajay even more broadly than before. Ajay didn't blink. The rain drummed a waterfall on the concrete.

"It is rare, all the rain we've been having," the man said. He

124

looked past Ajay and Madina to the street. "It is still very early, summer not yet here. We've already had many storms like this."

A gust of wind washed through the store and Ajay shivered, his T-shirt drenched.

"I like the rain," Madina said.

Ajay sipped his tea, and kept his eyes on the shopkeeper, who prattled on about the rain, directing his words mostly at Madina, while smiling at her in a way that made Ajay want to block her from the shopkeeper's view. Ajay shifted his eyes to a crack on the counter, then to the label on a can of fish. His head turned, and his eyes settled on Madina.

Hair clung to her shoulders. Black roots. A drop of water dripped from her right eyelash onto her cheek. He wanted to put his hand there, to collect the water on a fingertip and draw the gem to his mouth.

Ajay cleared his throat so harshly the shopkeeper's shoulders jumped. He cleared his throat, too.

"And what have you seen in Casablanca?" the man said.

"Plenty, but we haven't spotted Rick yet," Ajay said.

The shopkeeper popped a high laugh and followed with a torrent of lower warbling. "Another fan of that silly 'Casablanca' movie," the man said.

"It's not a silly movie," Ajay said.

The shopkeeper laughed. "Not to some people, apparently. Forgive me for not introducing myself. I am Hadj Brahim."

Ajay opened his mouth to say his name, but paused. Then he said, "I'm Timir. And this is my lovely wife, Bansari."

Madina dropped her eyes to the floor.

"In my language, Bansari means 'flute,'" Ajay said and gave the shopkeeper a wide smile. "It's funny, yes? My wife's name means flute and here she actually plays the flute."

"A musician?" the shopkeeper said. He jumped off his stool and clapped his hands.

"That's right. And she's one of the finest musicians I've ever played with," Ajay said. "We earned almost two hundred *dirham* today alone right here in this city."

The shopkeeper's eyes bounced from Ajay to Madina and back.

"Two hundred *dirham*! So you are a musician, too?" he said.

Ajay hoisted his drum bag for inspection.

Hadj Brahim held his hands out, palms up. "You must come with me tonight," he said. "I am from the south and every year my people, all the ones who live in Casablanca, hold a big festival with music and dancing. Tonight is that festival. You come as my guests. You won't be allowed to play on stage, but perhaps you could play outside for the crowd there. People wander in and out all evening. Now I have to close." The shopkeeper pressed a button on the register and the machine clicked an electronic tally while Hadj Brahim counted the money in the drawer.

"Dancing and music," Ajay said, his eyes on the money. "And refreshments, I suppose?"

"Oh, yes," the shopkeeper said. He put the money in a pouch and disappeared into the back room.

Ajay winked at Madina. "I think we should go to that festival."

She pulled a strand of hair out of her face. "My name is not Bansari. It's Madina." Though her tone held no threat, the statement unnerved him.

"All right," Ajay said.

The shopkeeper reappeared with a coat in hand. He looked towards Madina and pointed a finger at her, his expression solemn.

"I knew you were a musician when I first saw you," he said. "There is power in you."

CHAPTER 17

Six women danced onstage. All wore long dresses of green and had their black hair piled into tall hats on their heads. Their motions matched the frantic music, making the heavy gold and silver jewelry on their ears, necks and wrists a constant rush of jangle. The singer imparted his verses with closed eyes while a male chorus chanted in the background.

The high-ceilinged hall was white, bright and noisy with shouting from the enthusiastic crowd, the men dressed in their formal white *djellabah*. People walked in, walked out, greeted one another, laughed, the hour past midnight. Ajay scanned the faces of fathers, mothers, children, his stomach full of tea and cookies for which he'd paid nothing. He'd already seen and talked with the shopkeeper, who'd walked off to greet friends, leaving Ajay free to move among the chaos. To see what opportunities for theft arose, because one should never pass up an opportunity to earn. That and when they arrived in America, he would give Madina her fair share of whatever he collected.

He sat next to Madina, her mood evident in the way she leaned forward and watched the dancers and singers, her lips parted. Waiting for something portentous to happen, or something she could make happen. Though she was running out of time. six hours and they'd be on the ship.

The sluggish air smelled both sweet and humid, like a bakery where the scent of freshly baked goods mingled with that of customers' sweat. The dance ended and people stood and stretched.

Someone threw open the doors and cooler air wafted in. Spectators entered and exited before the next act. Ajay rose.

"Let's go," he said. Madina stood, eyes lingering on the stage, yet she followed Ajay to the doors. She'd been silent all evening. Not a sullen silence, but rather one that implied there was nothing else to say.

Outside Ajay looked at the night sky, but could see nothing due to a fog that had lowered. He took off his backpack and pulled out his wool sweater against the cool air. Where could they sleep for a few hours? He didn't want to venture into the surrounding medina, considering the old part of the city was a knot of narrow, dark streets. Yet sleeping down by the docks didn't sound safe, either.

He pulled the sweater over his head. While he shoved his arms through the sleeves, the whispery sketch of a face appeared in the fog. The shape grew in depth and detail until the face became full, real, that of an old woman, the plane of her eyes, mouth and nose sunken like a shallow bowl. The woman had long white hair and a thin neck of flabby skin. Her upper arms were ringed by bands of gold and she wore a red robe that wrapped around her like a sari. An apparition that had solidified in two seconds, maybe three. The type of ghost to capture Madina's imagination.

With smooth, quick steps, the old woman sailed to Madina and clamped a hand on her arm.

"It is good? All this?" the old lady said to Madina in a high voice rapid in its undulations.

But Ajay stepped up fast and so close he could have kissed the mole on the old woman's left cheek.

"What do you want?" he said.

The old woman kept her eyes on Madina.

"Music and dancing and dancing and music," the woman said in a trilling chattiness. "So *civilized*. But there is better. Yes, better."

"Madina," Ajay said. "Come."

"Yes, come, Madina," the old woman said. She lifted a hand and stroked Madina's arm. "Come with me to a private festival of ancient people." The woman took Madina's wrist. Ajay caught the other.

"Not this time," he said. "This time you're staying."

Madina pulled her hand. He tightened his grip.

128

"It's all right," she said.

"No it's not," Ajay said.

The old lady dropped Madina's wrist and laughed with her mouth closed. How funny would she find a slap on the face? Instead, Ajay looked down at where Madina held his free hand. That she would reach for him now, when it had always been the other way. In the desert when he touched her forehead to quiet her nightmared mind. In Marrakech when he lifted her foot to put on the sandal. Tonight as he clutched her wrist. The sensation of reaching out nothing compared to that of being sought.

"In the hotel today, a wind came," Madina said.

"*Bakvas*! I *knew* it," Ajay said.

She let go of his hand, the emptiness and cold sudden. "It told me to wait and watch for change and at first I thought…"

"Couldn't the wind have meant for me to save you?" he said.

Madina shook her head again.

"We're not going with her," Ajay said. "She could lead us to thieves."

"Then we'll be at home," Madina said. She smiled, then the smile was gone. "You should stay."

"*I* should stay? Why don't we both stay and let the old lady go for us?" he said.

The old lady laughed and put a hand on Madina's elbow. To lead her away from him. As if that would be easy.

Ajay loosened his grip on Madina's wrist, but didn't let go. "Now that I've had a chance to consider, I've decided to go with her. We have six hours in which to amuse ourselves and this sounds so educational." He walked at the old woman's heels as she led them away into the fog.

The old woman led Madina and Ajay into the old section of the medina where crumbling walls rose on either side of narrow, twisting streets. The three turned and turned again, right and left and right, left, left, a pattern nonexistent. Ajay tried to memorize their route, but soon everything looked the same. Dark, inset doors, shuttered windows, narrow alleys.

They turned a corner and the old woman walked to a black, closed door and knocked. Ajay stood back, his body loose, ready to respond. He'd let them enter first, then he'd check the room. Locate the exits. Count the people and determine if they had any weapons.

The door opened and Ajay heard music. The old woman entered first, followed by Madina. Ajay stopped just inside the door and blinked, the room bright with candlelight and filled with women, men, incense. But what caused his mouth to open and eyes to widen was that the room seemed dipped in gold. The walls, ceiling, floor a treasure chest of heat and glitter. Even the rug had streaks of gold woven through, and was the gold on the walls paint or gold leaf? And if real, could the soft metal be flaked off without anyone noticing?

A wide border of black letters, webbed and dripping delicacy, were painted around the top of the walls. Though what they said, Ajay didn't know because they weren't Arabic. The room's one small window was covered with a heavy curtain and barred from easy access by the men and women who stood against the wall and sat knee-to-knee on the floor. The hallway ahead of him ended in darkness, which would make looking for an escape hazardous, especially if he and Madina had to run.

When Madina took a step forward, Ajay held her arm to keep her near the front door. She stopped, but continued to lean forward, apparently willing to follow deep into this place if he let her. Yet the music drew him, too, the melody a seeking with the undertone of futility. Quite beautiful, but hardly something that would make people want to toss their coins.

Ajay scanned the crowd. Most of them were dressed in brightly-colored clothes and sat cross-legged on the floor. Many swayed, while some tapped their knees to the rhythm, their gazes never drifting from the men at the head of the room. One shook a tambourine hard enough to shake the walls, while the other man sat playing the one-stringed *rebab*, the sound like a child's wailing. Ajay lifted to his toes and craned his neck, but he didn't see a bowl, much less a square of cloth.

A female walked to Madina's side, leaned close and talked in a low voice Ajay couldn't hear over the music's sharp edge. The woman stood on the other side of Madina and sideways to Ajay, and because she wore a headscarf, he could only see her nose and mouth and the tip of her eyelashes. Yet there was something familiar about her, especially the mouth.

Ajay leaned closer and listened harder, but could hear nothing. He moved closer still, until his chest almost touched Madina's shoulder. The woman talked about how her people used to worship at the ancient temples. How they were driven away by invaders, yet nothing could make them stay away and one day they would rule again. A story all religious nuts told themselves.

The woman talked on. She was older, but not old, given the black strands of hair that curled around the edges of the scarf. She wore a red robe and smiled as she talked. A smile small and secretive. Like the bartender at the white and gold hotel. The woman glanced at Ajay, and he saw that she was. That woman. The bartender. But whereas the woman's eyes had been distant then, they now shone in a knowing way, one that matched a smile that said she knew all along who Madina was and where she would end up tonight.

The woman looked past Madina to Ajay. "Would you like to know what they're singing about?"

Without waiting, without allowing time for an escape, she pulled him into the story of an orphan. Like him. Like Madina. Though this orphan girl lived in a great city long ago. She was a beautiful girl with dark eyes and the smile of a princess bestowing mercy on the doomed. Small of body, light of limb, she could move like a bird, so fast she seemed to fly. No one knew where she came from or how she survived. Only that by the age of sixteen, she'd grown beautiful enough that sooner or later the king's scouts would see her and report back to him and he'd take her as a wife. People speculated about when that day would come. But then the girl vanished.

The king loved war. And because he loved war and pursued it to a victorious end time and time again, he grew powerful and his name became feared in surrounding lands. To keep his armies big and strong, the king constantly searched for soldiers. The more wars he instigated, however, the more soldiers died. The king's armies shrank and weakened while his subjects whispered their discontent at having lost so many sons and brothers and fathers. The more battles were lost, the louder and bolder the criticism grew.

The king was furious, but knew the danger of his peoples' rising anger. So the king dressed himself like a beggar and made a visit to an old woman he knew had come from the mountains of his mother's birth. The old woman was said to have a gift that was also a curse. She could see into the hearts of men.

The king asked the woman how he could recruit more soldiers from among those who now doubted him. The woman told him that within each heart was a spirit that allowed a person to know himself. Steal the spirit and the person would be lost and so follow without question.

But how do I steal the spirit from a man, let alone many men? the king asked.

The same way you steal anything, the old woman said. You hire a thief.

She directed him to a thief, who was not a *he* at all, but rather a *she*, and no more than a girl, at that. Although the king doubted she could steal anything, much less the spirits of men, he did as instructed and paid the orphan girl the gold she requested. Then he left. When he arrived in his kingdom, he sent out a call for soldiers and many signed on. He put out another call and received still more. For many years the king's armies were full and strong, ready to do his bidding.

Then one day the king called for soldiers and received only a small handful of men. Angered, he sent forth guards to determine the whereabouts of his thief of spirits. They returned and told him there was no sign of the girl. A rumor grew that the girl was now a beautiful, rich woman who had sailed across the water to a land of jungles.

The years passed. Many people assumed the thief died in that foreign land. But some believed she couldn't die because she'd never been human. They said she was a spirit who, though she could assume human form, preferred to roam the earth as a wind. That wherever she went, she stole the spirits of men.

The bartender smiled at Ajay. The room came back, the music, the people, the smell of ocean breeze. He looked at Madina. Her eyes wandered the room. Over all that gold.

CHAPTER 18

The sky shone of dim stars in a shade of night that every moment grew lighter. The outlines of the huge ships moored along the pier changed from the abstract to the distinct. Ajay and Madina meandered along the crumbling walkway. Soon the hull of the freighter they would board loomed above them. Though now arrived, now no more than an hour until departure, Ajay paced, his right fingers playing a rapid drum beat on his thigh. He shivered against the relentless sea breeze, constant in its chill. When he passed Madina for the third time, he stopped and followed her gaze up to the tall, dark towers from which the pilot would guide the ship to New York City five days away. Five days, meaning four nights in a small cabin with Madina. Close enough he could smell her and listen to her breathing and study her fingernails, yet far enough he could never reach her.

Ajay ground his teeth. "Well, did you learn anything?" he said.

"About what?" Madina said.

"During that meeting of crazy people. In the room of gold."

Madina didn't answer.

"I didn't think so." Ajay rubbed his hands together. When they got to New York he'd check the cost of transportation. Getting money wouldn't be a problem. A city like that would be crowded with wealthy people, but the competition would be steep. American criminals carried guns, or if they didn't, beat their victims. His own method of choice was to be quiet, light, subtle.

"Sometimes you have to think about something for awhile before it makes sense," Madina said.

A moment passed before Ajay focused on what Madina had said. He leaned toward her so far his bead necklace hung loose.

"And sometimes," he said, "you should calculate the risk before heading into danger." He straightened. "It was a good thing I was there to pull you away before you got brainwashed or robbed."

He paced again, stopping to kick stones into the water. Though the meeting had taken place only hours ago, the event seemed a nightmare of still-present sensations. Humid air, golden walls, the feeling of suffocation. The bartender's voice still whispering in his ear, the story nonsensical, yet disturbing. When she'd finished, Ajay took Madina's wrist, backed up, opened the door and pulled her out. She didn't resist, which meant she must have heard something she liked. Something she could turn into a clue.

They'd wandered for an hour through the narrow streets without speaking, trying to find a way out. Then Madina stopped and lifted her face, saying the wind would lead them to the ocean. He'd protested, but she ignored him and walked on. Another hour and they were at the harbor.

Ajay stopped and rubbed his eyes. When he got to the cabin, he'd sleep for a whole day. One day less in which he wouldn't have to think about his proximity to Madina. He studied the thick ropes that tied the freighter to the pier, then arched his neck to see the cranes that arced overhead. Vultures guarding a dead carcass. The seagulls circled. The water smelled of fish, garbage and oil. Crates the size of train cars towered in stacks on the freighter's deck. Ajay sniffed and jogged his shoulders into a short run.

"Quite a coincidence, don't you think?" he said, "That the storyteller turned out to be the bartender from the hotel?"

"I don't believe in coincidences," Madina said.

"Well I'm glad to hear that, because neither do I. I think she followed us. As a bartender, she must be good at spotting an easy mark."

"I don't think so."

"What? You think it was fate that we ran into her?"

"Yes."

"Then again I ask you, what did you get from that meeting? What morsel of information? What nugget of wisdom?"

Madina remained silent.

"There's no such thing as fate," Ajay said. "Everything just happens, all of it random, which I suspect is somewhere between coincidence and fate." He bounced on the balls of his feet to keep his legs warm, whereas Madina's didn't move. She kept her eyes on the ship. While she was so occupied, he let his eyes pause on her breasts before continuing to her face. Her eyes were waiting for him, his surprise so great his shoulders jumped. Well he wouldn't feel guilty. Let her see his lust. She didn't trust him anymore, not after that story about love being no more than a habit, so what did he have to lose? Let her see the truth, and all of it.

"Like when I met you," he said. "You were climbing, do you remember? You were climbing and I just happened to come along at that moment. Had I come even twenty minutes later, you would have been out of sight. Gone."

"But you came at the right time."

"But I might not have."

"But you did."

Ajay turned. He squinted at the Casablanca skyline, the orange and pink lighting the city's distant minaret. He shrugged his shoulders again and felt the horn's tip poke him in the back. He swung the backpack off and pulled out the animal horn. He held the horn out to Madina. She stepped back, her eyes wide and mouth open.

"You don't want it, yes?" Ajay said. "Well neither do I. It's always poking me in the back." He turned sideways and held the horn out over the edge of the pier.

"Wait," Madina said.

Ajay looked over his shoulder at Madina. "Why? It's deep enough."

"You don't know that. We need to be sure."

Ajay swung around to her. Again he offered her the horn. The tip pointed at her neck, like the knife she'd once held to his throat. The same knife with which she'd killed her mother then been forced by Old Aunt to cut vegetables with. Either use the knife or don't eat, the old camel had said. So Madina stopped eating. On the eighteenth day she wandered into the desert and climbed the cliff for what was supposed to be the first and last time. Because that was what Madina told him, that she climbed with the intent to throw herself off the top, this child who had murdered her mother. But the wind came, Madina had said. The wind wrapped its arms around her so she couldn't jump. And from then on, the wind had protected her.

"I'm tired of carrying this thing," Ajay said. "Of pretending it can end the world. If you don't want to dump it, you carry it. Whatever I'm doing now, consider it coincidence, fate, a random act, whatever you want, which is what you always do, anyway, yes? Interpret things however you want, in whichever way suits your story."

Madina kept her eyes on the horn. She didn't move.

Ajay turned toward the edge of the pier, though more slowly this time. Drawing Madina's eyes with him. He again held the horn out over the water.

"Wait," she said. She stepped forward. She licked her lips, reached out, and with an index finger and thumb, took the horn by its tip. Her hand shook, making the horn quiver. She shoved the instrument through an opening in her pouch, then tucked the bundle into the crook of her arm. Madina lifted her eyes to his. Even now, though he'd forced her to accept the instrument she believed could end the world, she didn't seem angry. What did he have to do to incur her wrath? To wake her up?

Madina whipped her head to the left. Ajay shot his glance that way, too, and listened. For footsteps, yells, anything that sounded like trouble. He heard nothing except water lapping at the pilings. But then he heard something, too, a low tremor that grew to voices. Low, male, distant, though not distant enough. He swept his gaze up the pier and down, but couldn't see anyone. The voices faded.

"What did that name mean," Madina said. "The new one you picked for yourself?"

But Ajay didn't answer. He watched, listened. Until he was sure there was no sound. Yet he continued to frown.

"Timir," Ajay said, his tone hushed, lest his voice carry to the people who had been talking. "It means *darkness*."

"How long before we board?" she said.

"Soon." Ajay leaned over the edge of the pier into the water

136

around the hull, the wind loose and swirling. The ship was close and solid. Ajay had an urge to touch the hull, to reassure himself that what he saw was real, because he was so tired and the meeting and the wandering clung to him, a surreal mirage. If he took a small jump, he could touch the ship, but then he'd fall and disappear into the black as he had at the waterfall. Ajay stepped back. He heard the tinkle of bells. Madina moving away, farther out onto the pier, which at least had an end. A finite length. A manageable area to monitor. An isolation from other troublesome humans.

Yet still he said, "Don't go far." Maybe because he held the horn out over the water, which he shouldn't have, just as he shouldn't have blackmailed her into taking the instrument. But ever since he'd told her the rest of the story yesterday, about the woman losing her husband, the color of time felt wrong, bending where the hours and minutes should proceed in a straight line, deepening where they should be shallow. Everything connected to Madina seemed confusing, contradictory. Unlike assumptions and theories, facts held power due to their indisputable nature. One either survived or didn't. Won or lost. Such facts could be seen, felt, tasted, touched, heard, whereas confusion derived from the unseen. From opinions idiots mistook for fact.

The blue of the eastern sky mixed with the pink and orange of a dawn close at hand. Again he heard the bobbling of tones above the lapping water. The wind through his hair made his scalp shrivel, the touch so light. A whistle sounded, one made by human lips. A wakeup signal that came from far down the pier. Where Madina stood. With a man.

"*Bakvas*." Ajay shouldered his backpack, grabbed his drum bag and jogged down the pier. The man turned away from Madina and walked toward Ajay, head down. A man dressed in loose green trousers and heavy boots, a dirty white T-shirt and thick leather belt. Ajay slowed, expecting the man to stop, but the man strode past and without pausing, lifted his head and nodded at Ajay once. Though the man's hair was thick and black, his skin was light. He continued on his way.

Ajay walked to Madina, who stood before the gangplank of a ship a quarter the size of the freighter. The ship had a faded red and white exterior, a prominent smokestack and numerous crates on the

137

deck. A rooster crowed somewhere. A man yelled in a language Ajay didn't recognize. Goats and sheep bleated. Children laughed, the ship an unwashed old man still shouldering a too-large family.

The sun broke over the city's skyline. The brighter the light, the sorrier the ship appeared with its black, rusting hull, peeling white paint and deck crowded with animal pens. The pilot's room was only a single story high and the scent of cows and diesel fuel hung in the air.

And again the whistling, on-key and upbeat. A man stood up from behind one of the crates, his hair black, too, and nose large and crooked as a thumb. He held a wrench and continued to whistle while looking around for something, maybe a tool he'd misplaced. An older man squatted by the bow near an old woman dressed in black. Another old woman, when there had been too many already — the one who'd pulled him from an alley, Old Aunt, the festival witch — all of them intruding, pushing, condemning. This one resembled the ducks in the crate she sat on, what with her small head and rotund body. She wore her white hair pulled tight off her forehead and held her lips bunched, like she was ready to kiss someone. Three or four other men and a few boys. The engines rattled below.

A young man passed Ajay and strode up the gangplank. Madina asked the young man something in what sounded like French. The man, already five strides up the ramp, looked over his shoulder at her.

Madina asked again, though this time in Arabic. "Where are you going?" she said.

The young man jerked his head, indicating south, and talked in a language Ajay couldn't follow, except for the words *South America*.

Madina stepped forward. "Are there jungles there?" she asked in English.

"Jun-glays?" the man said.

"Yes, jungles," Madina said.

Jungles, jungles, a recent mention of jungles. But the weariness of the past several days, the walk across the desert, the waiting and the searching in the cities, weighed Ajay down so that thinking took effort. But when understanding came he almost leapt a step forward. He smiled and waved his burned and blistered hand at the young man.

"Never mind," Ajay said. "She's tired and doesn't know what she's talking about." He hooked his arm through Madina's and pulled back, but she leaned forward. Her feet didn't move.

"Come on, Madina." Ajay said, tugging harder. That she would do this to him. "It's time to go."

The old duck lady in black spoke from her seat on the deck. "Jungle?" she said in English.

Madina nodded. "Trees," she said and raised her arm to indicate how tall. "And birds, monkeys. Rain and heat. Jungle."

"South America?" The old lady nodded. "Yes."

Ajay gripped Madina's arm, his thumb pressing into the hollow of her tightened muscle. "Our ship is leaving."

"But this one goes to jungles," Madina said. Eyes bright on the shores of a land thousands of kilometers away. To jungles, the hiding place of women who stole men's souls.

"You can't do this," Ajay said.

"A place of jungles," she said.

Ajay yanked Madina around to face him. "You think that's what that crazy woman's story was about?" he said. "That you're supposed to go to a jungle? That that's where this war of winds will happen?"

"Yes, yes."

"And what about me?" Ajay blurted. "I'm a storyteller, too. What if I tell you your war is with me, in America. That I've got limits and you've passed them. Passed them all, and now you owe me."

"But a jungle," Madina said, her eyes climbing up him. Searching for a handhold, a foothold, a way inside. "Are there jungles in America?"

"Yes!" he yelled.

"Really?"

"Probably."

"You've never been there."

The old lady laughed. "We have room," she said in English.

Madina turned her face to the woman. "How much?"

Ajay couldn't squeeze Madina's arm any tighter, and still she didn't grimace. She didn't look like he touched her at all, or had ever touched her. He flung her arm away.

"I've waited too long for this," he said.

"Then go," Madina said.

"You would do that? Send me away?"

"You want a bride, a home. We must each do what we must do. I understand."

"You don't! You don't understand anything." Ajay turned away, a hand to his forehead. His new home in America. A place to store his drums for good.

The old woman was speaking, going on about how her nephew broke his leg and he and his family had to stay in Greece.

"So two rooms," the old lady said. "They just go to waste."

"Stay. Your ship—" Madina said.

"*Our* ship, and don't keep telling me to stay, to stay!" Ajay said.

The old lady laughed, a sound young and high in its trilling.

"But I'm supposed to go," Madina said.

"Well I'm supposed to go with you, or did you forget?" Ajay said.

Madina bit her lip. She hadn't forgotten, then, yet she encouraged him to stay.

"Why are you trying to get rid of me?" Ajay said.

"We must each do what we must do," Madina said.

Ajay opened his mouth and made a sound. A cough. A choke. Somewhere in between. He turned in a circle and stopped to scratch his ear. He looked down at his feet, at his boots, so long on the travel. Someone else approached. When Ajay lifted his head, he saw a large, flabby man standing next to Madina, a foreigner with blond hair and white skin the color of *samosa* dough. The man had a wide, smiling mouth of tiny, yellowed teeth. His small blue eyes peered from behind thick lenses of silver wire-frame glasses.

"Hello," the man said in Arabic.

When neither Madina nor Ajay spoke, the man leaned toward the ship and squinted at the name on the hull. When he saw the old woman, he talked in what must have been her native language, because her speech flowed without effort. The man nodded and smiled.

"Once again, I arrive just in time," he said. He looked from Ajay to Madina. "Are you coming aboard?"

Again Madina and Ajay said nothing.

The man nodded once. "Cheap passage, that's what I look for. That and the chance to get to my destination on time. In this case, that means meeting a friend in Buenos Aires by the end of the month." The man smiled. "Right. Well, if you'll excuse me," and he walked up the gangplank.

Now that the man had gone aboard, only one room would be available. One room on this vessel with Madina, or one alone on the freighter.

"You would go without me," Ajay said.

Madina rolled her lower lip beneath the upper. When she released them, they bloomed. Full and lush.

"Do you want me to leave?" Ajay said.

She reached out. With her palm to him, she patted his forehead. His weariness bled away. His mind stilled. She lowered her hand. His gaze floated toward the ship. He shook his head.

"I think we're going to drown in this thing, along with the roosters and chickens," Ajay said.

The old lady in black cackled a laugh from her perch above.

CHAPTER 19

Madina stood at the bow of the ship, her belly against the railing and face to the ocean. The wind blew her hair behind her and made the ends whip and snap. She wore a heavy, dark green coat the old woman had offered after dinner on this first night on the ship. Tremendous clouds billowed upward, darkening the horizon. The setting sun lit the clouds from behind with an explosion of orange and pink. The ship rose and fell on the rolling swells. Madina looked at the pouch clutched in her hand, then out at the blackening water, the time having come to bury the horn. The winds would find a way to start the war, but without her help. She leaned her right hip against the railing, reached into the cloth bag and slid her hand around the instrument.

"Hello," a man said from behind.

Madina turned. The foreigner with the pale skin approached, one hand in the pockets of his gray trousers and the other out to steady himself. "My name is Henry Dawson," he said in Arabic. He smiled and put a hand on the railing.

Madina released the horn and drew her hand out of the pouch.

"I apologize for interrupting," Henry said. "It's just I've noticed how the bow seems to be your favorite place on the ship. I don't think I've ever seen anyone stand still for so long in a spot this exposed to the wind. It's a good thing you have a nice warm coat."

Madina raised her hand to the railing. "I like the wind. Most of the time."

Henry smiled and leaned against the railing. He crossed his

arms over his large chest. "I do, too. In fact, I collect stories about the wind, among other things."

Madina cocked her head. She stood with her back to the wind now, her hair flying forward. She used a hand to gather and hold the fury.

"Did you see the name on this ship?" Henry said.

Madina shook her head.

"Aeolus." He pushed his glasses farther up on his nose. "In Greek mythology, Aeolus was a god who lived on a floating island where the winds were kept. He was the warder, you see, which means he guarded the winds."

Henry took a handkerchief from his coat pocket and blew his nose. He folded the red and white handkerchief and returned the cloth to his pocket.

"In most stories," he said, "the winds are portrayed as unmanageable by human standards because they're huge, powerful, destructive. Yet it's the humans who triumph in the end, either by holding the winds in check or hurting them. Take Adapa in Babylonian lore. He broke the wings of the great south wind that overturned his fishing boat. Adapa's father, a god, thought his son's action impetuous so he tricked Adapa out of his inheritance, which was immortality."

"Did the south wind recover?" Madina said.

Henry laughed. "I don't know. I suppose it must have, though perhaps it learned a lesson from Adapa and stopped turning over fishing boats. It must have, because the Iroquois — a tribe of native people in America — described the south wind as soft as a fawn."

"What's a fawn?"

Henry smiled. "A baby animal with four long legs and soft fur – a baby deer."

Madina tucked her pouch farther into the crook of her arm. "What other wind stories do you know?"

Henry scanned the sky and exhaled. "There are thousands of stories about the wind and what forces control it."

"Tell me," she said.

The light of the sky dimmed and the ship lights came on as Henry told Madina of Notus, the southwest wind in Greek mythology. And Notus' brother, Boreas, who devoured the north wind. Of Shen Nung, the burning wind in Chinese lore, and Badessy in Haitian voodoo. The Hindu wind god, Indra, was a storm god that had four arms with which to throw thunderbolts at the earth.

"In Japanese lore, Susano, the storm god, had a sun goddess for a sister," Henry said. "While Susano could be good, he could also be sneaky. He once tricked his sun goddess sister into hiding in a cave, which plunged the world into darkness. It was a joke the other gods didn't think was very funny."

By now, he and Madina sat on the deck below the gunwale, which protected them against the wind and spray, the night a blunt, complete dark due to the clouds that hid the half moon. Beams from the lights on the stern stretched through the corridors of crates and cages on the deck.

"In Toltec mythology," Henry said, "there was a wind god who fought with his brother. At one point, out of revenge, the wind god swept the earth with a tremendous tornado and then replaced the sun god with a goddess that flooded the land, killing all humans and dousing even the sun and stars."

Madina sat up, her mouth open. She stared at Henry, who had taken off his glasses and now cleaned them with a handkerchief from his other pocket.

"That last story," he said, "it's really very similar to the one from the Judeo-Christian bible. Do you know it?"

Madina shook her head.

"Well, in that story — and this is a very loose interpretation — God seemed to feel he'd made a mistake by creating people and so decided to kill them off and try again." Henry put on his glasses and blinked a few times. "God asked a man and his wife to load a female and male of each animal species onto a ship and then get on the ship themselves. Then God used the wind and rain and lightning to flood the earth and drown everything left behind, his intent to create a new world."

Music could be heard, though vaguely, above the rumble of the ship's engines.

"It would be a terrible way to die, waiting to starve or drown," Madina said.

"I think it would, yes," Henry said. "I'd rather be killed quickly. I mean, if you knew something bad was going to happen and had the power to bring about a fast, merciful end for yourself, or more importantly, your loved ones, wouldn't you?"

Madina's eyes slid to the pouch, which held the horn, a terrible instrument that could destroy the world. Perhaps she should keep the horn. An instrument that could give her the power to bring an end to man's suffering, if she ever felt there was such a need. She clutched the pouch tighter in her arm.

CHAPTER 20

Ajay lay on the top bunk in the closet-sized cabin he and Madina shared. He had an arm thrown over his eyes and he'd strung the black bead necklace across his chin. He turned the beads over and over with the fingers of his other hand while waiting for her.

When the door opened, the small space floated in yellow from the hallway. Ajay remained still, his eyes closed. He heard Madina step inside and close the door. Darkness returned. He turned his face to where she should be, but could see nothing. She stood only a few paces from him, yet remained hidden. He heard the soft thump of her pouch on the metal chair, then the shaking off of the old lady's coat. Then he heard the whisper of sandals slipping off her feet, so that now she stood in her bare feet.

His body tensed. Then it came, the low *fffft* followed by a soft *wump*, sounds Ajay heard for the first time last night. Sounds that puzzled him until he realized their origin. She came in. She took off her coat, her sandals. Then she removed her blouse and skirt, the *fffft* from pulling the blouse over her head and the *wump* of her skirt dropping to the floor. She'd undressed before him, within arm's length. All he'd had to do was reach through the darkness and she would have been there, her skin, her hair. Her breath.

All day Ajay had wanted to ask her — yell at her — where she got the audacity to undress in front of him, even if cloaked in darkness? After all this time of traveling with him, why bother now to take off her clothes to sleep? Was the cabin too warm? Did her clothes tangle in the blankets? Or did she mean to torture him by turning his sleep into a mauling of frustrated desire?

Questions he dared not ask, because if she knew how he listened with such intensity, she might change her new habit and he might never again hear those soft, subtle sounds of cloth dropping to the floor. *Ffft* goes the blouse. *Wump* goes the skirt. Secret sounds that once found, a man couldn't do without.

Ajay swallowed. He opened his mouth wide to inhale so she wouldn't hear how she made him gulp air. He inhaled again, her scent coming to him. Of salt and sweat and the smell that belonged only to females.

The creak of her bed. The rustle of limb and sheet as she stretched out. The pull of blankets to cover her nakedness. Then quiet.

Ajay stared into the blackness, fingering the beads.

CHAPTER 21

"Pour me another," Ajay said. Henry smiled and poured another glass of the clear liqueur. The meal over, only three other men remained drinking strong Greek coffee in the ship's low-ceilinged mess hall. Madina had gone, her disappearance through one of the squat doorways on either side of the room no surprise. She'd been on deck for all but the six or seven hours a day necessary to sleep and eat.

Ajay glanced at the yellow walls made more hideous by the overhead lights. He sat at one of three long, scratched metal tables bolted to the floor. He breathed through his mouth so he wouldn't have to smell the remains of dinner mixed with that of dirty dishwater in the adjacent kitchen where those cleaning up laughed and chatted in a language he didn't understand. A thumping, soul-less music played in the background.

A piece of chalk hung by a long string beside a chalkboard outside the kitchen. Every time the ship rolled, the chalk swung in a wide arc. Ajay watched the pendulum grow wider and wider until he felt his dinner rise in his throat. He closed his eyes and groaned. When he opened them, they fell on the bottle of liqueur still on the table.

"Ouzo," he murmured. "It tastes exactly like poison should. Strong, bitter, with a terrible aftertaste and a horrible smell. Yet it won't kill me. Just one more case in which appearance means nothing. Not that I'm complaining."

Henry laughed. "Why do you drink it if you don't care for it?"

Ajay lowered his voice and glanced at the men at the next table before looking at Henry. "It's better than what I ate for dinner."

Henry laughed again. He was a champion laugher, this Henry. He laughed with his mouth of crooked teeth stretched wide. He laughed with his broad shoulders and his great belly and his small blue eyes. The laughter made his feathery blond hair flutter and his white skin blotch.

"What was it we ate, anyway?" Ajay said, glancing at the remains of dark green oiled leaves and a crumbling of grain, the thick smell of spice still prevalent. He looked away.

Henry shook his bangs from his eyes. "That was *dolmadhes*. Stuffed grape leaves."

At least ouzo could rid one's mouth of any taste, provided one drank enough. He rarely got drunk since doing so slowed both wit and action, leaving one vulnerable. That and now his dizziness was compounded by the rise and fall of the ship, the weather rough tonight.

Yet he had a good reason to be drunk, didn't he? He'd given up everything and now found himself stuck on a rickety vessel loaded with noisy animals, both human and otherwise, including two young grandchildren. There was little room to walk, no crowd from which to extract money and only one room to share with a woman who undressed in front of him without being seen.

Fortunately the God of Luck hadn't abandoned Ajay completely. One of the sailors named Danaos owned a guitar and in the evenings would play with Ajay while the others listened and clapped and the old woman, the traitor who'd told Madina about the jungles in South America, danced. She'd turned out to be the captain's mother. Occasionally Danaos' older brother would join the duo and play his accordion, an instrument that sounded like a monkey being skinned alive.

Ajay had tried to get Madina to play with him and Danaos several times, but she wouldn't leave her place on deck, though the ocean winds had stripped her skin raw. She endured the punishment even though she said the winds wouldn't talk to her. They were soldier winds, serious, directed and with no time to chat. So that all she could do was stand day after day and watch them race by while listening for fragments of what they said. From the way she talked about them, Ajay could tell she admired their strength and speed, even though they ignored her, whereas Ajay didn't ignore her. He was there, always there.

Ajay blinked. Danaos had gone, which was probably for the best, since Ajay couldn't play now if he wanted to. Not even the little grandchildren were about, the girl, Malina, and boy, Dimitris, who liked to hold a coin in his outstretched hand and dare Ajay to snatch the money, which he did every time. At least one person impressed by him.

Makhaon, the square-shouldered father of the two children, came in dressed in a wet slicker. He leaned through the mess hall door on the right side of the room and said something to the men still sitting at the tables, his words sharp and quick. The men stopped talking and rose.

"What does that mean, what Makhaon said? *Ela*?" Ajay said.

"*Come here.*" Henry lifted his face to the low ceiling. "Looks like we're in for a bit of a blow." Then Henry frowned. "It's funny, though."

"What is?"

"That we should be running into this weather," Henry said. "The sailors told me earlier a hurricane had developed far south of here. They didn't think we'd feel the effects all that much. Now it seems to be creeping up." Henry smiled. "Maybe it's following us."

The children's grandmother — a tiny, aged beauty, save for a large mole on her chin — strode out from the kitchen to collect the men's coffee cups. She never missed a step despite the movement of the ship. When she picked up Ajay's plate of unfinished food, she scowled at him and backhanded the air, then fired a volley of rapid talk while walking toward the kitchen.

"I've been meaning to tell you, you have a very interesting wife," Henry said. "She seems to be quite enamored of all things related to the wind."

"You've been talking to her?"

"Almost every evening while you're playing with Danaos and Nessos. She has a very keen mind."

Ajay found himself fingering his bead necklace. He dropped his hand to the table.

151

"When I learned of her interest in wind, I borrowed an old mariner's map from the captain," Henry said. "I spread it out and explained how the lines on the map represent winds. Like trade winds, for example." He paused. "She went perfectly silent for the longest time. It was really very extraordinary. I felt as though I had handed her a treasure map for which she'd been searching for years. She looked at the map and told me her names for the trade winds. Do you know what she calls them? Movers!" He smiled. "And then she asked an enormous number of questions."

Ajay leaned forward. "What kind of questions?"

"Anything about wind. About hurricanes and tornadoes, about what travels on the wind or gets propelled by it. Things like dust, hot air balloons, sailboats, parachutes, sound, that kind of thing."

"Sound?"

"Certainly. How the wind carries sound. We even—"

Ajay tried to sit up. "And she understood?"

"As I said, your wife has a very keen mind. We even talked about..."

Yesterday Ajay had asked Madina if she'd gotten rid of the animal horn. She'd said yes. Born to disbelieve, Ajay had waited for a chance to check her pouch. To be sure. But Madina took her pouch everywhere.

The room went silent. Henry had been talking, but now wasn't.

"What?" Ajay said.

"I said, we even talked about the Beaufort Scale of wind force." When Ajay didn't say anything, Henry explained that zero on the scale meant there was no wind, while twelve on the scale was a hurricane."

"What do you think we're at now?" Ajay said.

"Oh, I should say in the seven or eight range. Gale force. Though I doubt this ship could take more than ten." Henry nodded. "The truth is, I find wind interesting myself. I'm a folklorist, you see."

"What does working in a forest have to do with wind?"

Henry remained silent a moment, a surprised look on his face. Then he laughed. "A folklorist studies folk tales, which are more or less stories passed from one generation to the next."

"You're a storyteller?"

"More a collector of stories."

The ship rose, rolled to the right and fell, the hull coming down hard on the water's surface. Ajay's vision blurred. He swallowed and kept his unblinking eyes on the table, his hands gripping the surface. Trying not to throw up while at the same time trying to think. About why Madina would be interested in how the wind carried sound. Wondering why he had this feeling that Madina had not thrown the horn into the sea.

"A long time ago," Henry said, "women used to sell favorable winds to sailors…"

Ajay kept his eyes on the table. The horn. The pouch. But Henry's words floated in, bringing with them the image of women standing on a dock, taking a sailor's money in exchange for a blessing. Either way, the women won. If good winds followed the sailor, he'd return for another blessing, whereas if he got washed away in a storm, he couldn't ask for a refund.

Ajay laughed. "That's a good one, *filos*," he said, using the Greek word for *friend*. "A good one."

Though Henry's deep laugh ebbed, his smile didn't. "Sailors used to believe Finns could create favorable winds."

"What's a Finn?"

"A person from Finland. A northern country east of Sweden. Very cold."

The ship rolled. Ajay swallowed, the last of his smile disappearing. The pouch. The storm. Madina.

"So how did the Finns create wind? By blowing into the sails?" . The ship creaked and heeled to the side. He gripped the table to keep from falling backward. He looked at the ceiling.

"Unfortunately the Finns didn't receive kindness, much less monetary compensation," Henry said. "Instead of paying the Finn for his trouble, the seamen would kidnap him until he caused a favorable wind."

"Much cheaper."

"Yes."

The ship heaved and fell. A yelp rose from the kitchen. Henry stood, his head almost touching the ceiling. A young woman emerged, gripping the grandma under the arm while the grandma held a bloodied towel to her forehead. The two worked their way between the tables and toward the door. Henry talked to them in Greek. The grandma shook her head and waved a hand before exiting to the hallway that led to the cabins on the ship's starboard side.

Henry frowned and lowered back to the bench. "I suppose the best thing we can do now is to stay out of the way."

The ship heaved so hard Ajay slid sideways on the bench. He gripped the table tighter.

"Oh," Henry said.

"Oh, what?" Ajay said.

"I've just had a thought," Henry said. He looked at Ajay. "Do you suppose there's any chance your wife is still out on deck?"

"I don't know."

"I never even thought that someone might try to remain on deck during this kind of weather. But then your wife is extraordinarily fond of—" Henry stood. "I'll go look for her."

"*I'll* go look for her," Ajay said. He pushed himself up.

"Let me check her cabin first," Henry said. Three strides and he was gone.

Ajay got to his feet and walked to the exit, stumbling right then left. He leaned in the doorway a moment and heard Henry's voice calling from behind.

"She's not in your cabin," he yelled.

Ajay turned to Henry, who peered through the opposite doorway. Ajay nodded and swiveled his head back, though slowly so his vision wouldn't blur.

"Perhaps I should come with you," Henry said.

"No."

"Well, why don't you wait here a moment," Henry said. "I'll make a check of all the cabins and then call up to the captain. Just to make sure she's not somewhere else."

When Henry left, Ajay stepped into the hallway leading to a flight of steep, narrow stairs up to the deck. The door at the top of the stairs was shut. Ajay climbed, his shoulders bouncing from wall to wall as he went. He fell forward, hitting his shins against the top step. He gripped the railing with a hand and cursed. The ship reared. The bow came down hard. Ajay crawled the last few steps with his teeth clenched. He tried to push the door open, but couldn't. He lodged one foot on the top step and one against the opposite wall. He pushed on the door with his shoulder. The ship plunged down. The door flew open.

Ajay rolled onto the deck, his body at once drenched in chilly saltwater and rain. He pushed to his knees in the yellow light of the spotlights that lit the deck, which was now empty of all crates and animal pens. The ship lifted. When the vessel dropped, Ajay flattened himself against the deck so he wouldn't roll again. Water surged over the bow, covering him. He spluttered and coughed. The roar of wind filled his head and jags of lightning splintered. Thunder boomed. The rain flew sideways. The ship rose and dropped again and Ajay slid farther out. When he stopped sliding, he pushed to his hands and knees and crawled toward the door, but the wind was a train that drove him backward. He couldn't see well for the water in his eyes. He glanced up to get his bearings. The sky flickered with lightning. In that moment he saw her, Madina. She stood on a rung of the ladder leading to the pilot's tower, her arms hooked behind her through the metal frame and her face outward. She appeared to be screaming something towards the sky, but the words were drowned out by the water, wind and the crash of thunder.

There was another, longer, flash of lightning, one in which Ajay saw everything about Madina. The black hair snaking around her neck. The eyes almost lightning white and raised in rapture toward the roiling sky. She appeared to be screaming something. Though her words were inaudible, drowned out by the sound of the storm, the expression on her face was unequivocal and terrifying. It proclaimed that she would give up everything and everyone to fulfill her duty in stopping the war of winds.

CHAPTER 22

Ajay lay quietly in his bunk, facing the wall. He still wore a bandage on his forehead and another around his wrist from his injuries the night of the storm. Several smaller bandages on his legs covered the gashes where the edges of the stairs had cut him when he fell down the stairs while trying to get off the deck. His neck was bare, the black bead necklace hanging from a corner of the bunk. He listened to the occasional click of beads against metal as the ship rose and fell in now-modest swells.

Madina had come in off the deck a few minutes before. He listened to her clothes dropping, but not with desire this time. Only dread. Dread of this maniacal, black hole of a woman who could scream defiance in the face of catastrophe and draw everyone down with her.

Madina stirred in her bunk. "Ajay, there's something I need to tell you."

Ajay tensed, but did not reply.

"There's something I need to tell you," she said. "Are you listening?"

"*Utrukiini,*" he said. *Leave me alone.*

"When we get off the ship you cannot come with me."

Ajay felt a surge of anger that almost made him shout out at Madina. After she had caused him to miss his chance for a new life in America, just to follow her. And here she was, tossing him aside like a handful of sand scooped up in the desert. But this made matters simpler. Saved him from having to explain to her he'd already made up his mind they could not continue together. She had already caused

157

him enough damage. He had been deluding himself that he could guide Madina away from her strange obsession with the winds and their war. And then that glimpse of her, screaming into the storm… if he didn't escape her — didn't part with her as soon as they went ashore in Argentina —she'd sooner or later sacrifice him. She wouldn't mean to, but she would, anyway.

Ajay had said his goodbyes the night before. To Danaos and his accordion-playing brother. To the kids, the cooks, the grandma with the bandage on her forehead at the hairline and the old lady in black. Now Ajay walked out of the Customs house and onto the pier in the port of Buenos Aires. Henry said there would be a festival going on in celebration of cattle and the beef dishes would be delicious, a true carnivore's delight. But would there be big crowds? Ajay had asked. Most assuredly, Henry said. So today Ajay would make money. A thought that would have once thrilled him, whereas now all he wanted was enough. Enough to buy food. Enough to occasionally afford a bus or train ride. He'd work his way north, though there was no hurry now. Because he'd missed his deadline. He'd failed to reach his destination on time and the opportunity had almost certainly evaporated.

So Ajay would take Henry's advice and try the *empanadas,* and drink *mate* made from some Paraguayan herb Ajay couldn't remember. And he'd visit the *Casa Rosada* in the *Plaza de Mayo,* because why not? He'd be here for at least a few days. Maybe he could even see a movie. Henry had been so impressed when Ajay said he'd seen the classic Argentinean movie *La Casa del Angel* that he didn't mention how he liked gaucho movies better.

Ajay walked up the pier, wearing his backpack and holding the drum bag in his mostly healed right hand. Though the breeze was cool, the sun felt warm. Sea birds screeched overhead.

A man called Ajay's name.

He turned. Henry had just exited the Customs house and was walking towards Ajay. Henry smiled, the expression in his eyes half embarrassed, half troubled. He glanced around, no doubt wondering at the whereabouts of Ajay's *wife.*

"Off, are you?" Henry said.

Ajay nodded. "What about you?"

"I'm meeting some friends." Henry adjusted the duffel bag hooked over his right shoulder. "Right. Well, take care of yourself."

He walked away, but after some twenty paces, turned back and called to Ajay.

"Your wife," he said. "She really is most unusual." His mouth opened as if to say more, but then he only said, "Well, take care...." He waved a hand and walked away.

When Henry had walked to a distance that made him look half his size, Ajay shouted, "Thanks to you, *filos*, the next time I go on a ship I'll know to kidnap a Finn first."

Henry turned, and walking backward smiled, waved a hand and walked on. Ajay's smile faded with every step Henry took until both disappeared.

Ajay stood where he was, looking down at the pier's planking, feeling vaguely disturbed. He heard the bells before the footsteps. His left shoulder jerked in that direction, but he stopped himself. Step, jingle, step, jingle. The footsteps came closer until they threatened to walk over him. But Madina passed him without a glance, walking as she normally did with her feet slightly turned out, head down and pouch tucked in the crook of her arm. Her skirt whipped about her calves in the ocean wind. Soon she was ten paces away, then fifteen. Now twenty.

Ajay's hand tightened on his drum bag. He swallowed, his eyes tearing from the sharp wind, yet he didn't blink. He stared at the woman now far down the pier. The crazy woman who climbed like a spider and ran through her dreams, terrified. Who'd shed the robe, the headscarf, and let cloth slip from her shoulders when immersed in the dark. She was now so far away he couldn't see or hear the tinkle of her ankle bracelet. Half-sized and shrinking fast. A ship's horn sounded.

"No!" he said, his teeth grit. He whipped his head right, left, to see if anyone dared contradict him, but no one watched. No one cared. Ajay returned his eyes to the now small figure. Soon he could no longer see her skirt swishing, Madina reduced to only basic colors. Yellow, black, blue, a bruise. She reached the place where the pier met the land. In a moment she'd turn the corner and like Henry, would be gone.

This woman who defied a killer storm. Who could frighten the hardest criminal. This woman of slim ankles, thin wrists and a face made forever calm by the home she carried with her, a world that could swallow one whole. But rich, so rich, a haven of gold that no true thief could resist.

"*Bakvas!*" he said. He picked up his drum bag and jogged. "Madina," he yelled, then again. He ran, trying to keep the small figure in focus. Madina was almost around the corner.

"Madina*!*"

Madina disappeared.

Ajay put his head down and ran. His right shoulder ached from holding the drum bag away from his body. His legs ached. When he looked up, he had to brake hard or run into Madina, who stood less than an arm's length away as she had on the first day they met. Startling in detail. Face abloom with color. She waited, her eyes on him. Not on the people along the avenue behind her, the cars on the road. She looked at him with her habitual far-away look, as if she was seeing something that was worlds away.

Ajay stood, gasping. But even when his breathing slowed, no words came. His eyes fell to her feet. His hand slipped into his pants pocket and he fingered the bead necklace, the one he'd meant to leave on the ship, but couldn't.

When he looked up, her green eyes were on him. Still. Weight sheered from his mind, leaving his thoughts clear and light. His breathing calmed. His neck no longer ached. He straightened his shoulders and stood taller. This was the third time he'd had to run after Madina, and the last, because he had nowhere else to go.

He smiled.

"You can't come," Madina said.

The smile fell away. "Why not?"

"Because if you stay with me, the winds will kill you. I can't allow that."

"Me in particular?"

"Yes."

"Why do they want to hurt me?"

"I'm not sure yet."

"Then we'd better ask."

160

CHAPTER 23

Ajay stood by the dirt road in southern Brazil next to Felix, the German climber who'd given Ajay and Madina a ride to this place of rock pinnacles and little else. Ajay stood even with the man's bicep, Felix maybe two meters tall. Wisps of brown hair escaped the pink and green tie-dyed scarf around his head and a goatee sprouted from his dimpled chin. He stood shirtless with hands on his hips, his body thin and muscled. He didn't wear sunglasses to shield his blue eyes, and so squinted at where Madina climbed. She had reached the midpoint of a pinnacle about twenty meters away across a field of grass and wildflowers that rippled in a warm breeze. She wore the same loose pants and sleeveless shirt in which Ajay had first seen her, and again she resembled a spider, her arms and legs outstretched and her skin brown against the pale gray rock. Ajay strained to see her in the glare from a sky filled with long, torn clouds. He scratched the back of his neck under the black bead necklace.

Besides the German, about twelve other climbers stood along this rural road, their vehicles parked nearby. Some leaned on their cars and squinted at Madina while others looked through binoculars. The German wandered up and down, stopping to point and talk about her.

He'd talked for almost the entire three-hour drive to this locale. About rope brands and anchors, lines and gobis. About fist jams, slabs, laybacking and harnesses. He mentioned the need to smear this and mantle that and the urge to dyno for dynoing's sake.

161

And though he sometimes rubbed chalk on his hands, should he, considering the chalk left blotches on the rock that ruined its natural appearance? Yet if he didn't use chalk on certain types of rock, his hands might slip.

But at least the German had relieved Ajay and Madina of silence. Where she had bloomed in Marrakech and Casablanca, she'd grown quiet again, back to her desert demeanor. Thinking, and maybe doubting now, too.

"I've come out here for the last two days just to study my route," the German said. "Yet here is your wife. She comes, she looks at it and she starts to climb. No book, no advice from other climbers, no idea of the route she'll take. And that she's going to scale over a hundred meters without a rope!" The German shook his head and crossed his arms over his chest. "It is unbelievable."

Felix smiled, his eyes on Madina, who was some forty meters above the ground now. He threw an arm out toward the cliff summit. "If she gets to the top, how will she get down? She will have to climb down. Think how tired she will be. I can't believe you let her climb without a rope, without shoes, even. If she was my wife—"

"She is not your wife," Ajay said.

If the German heard the sharpness, he didn't seem to care.

"She climbs well, though," the German said. Then he looked Ajay up and down. "Do you climb?"

"No."

"Well, you see how she keeps her weight over her feet? So as not to make her arms tired? I have seen so many amateur climbers try and pull themselves up, the idiots. She has been climbing a long time, I think."

Ajay kept his mouth shut tight and his eyes on Madina.

"She is agile and flexible," the German said. "She keeps her feet still until she knows where to put one, and then the other. See how she feels the rock? Sweeps it, looking for edges and pocket grips along that central crack. It is a favorite line she's taking and one I may take, myself. You see how it leads to a narrow shelf halfway? But the top portion is tricky because of the chickenhead."

"The chickenhead?" Ajay said.

"It is a—" and the man cupped both of his broad, muscled hands, "—rounded section of stone. She will have to pull herself up

162

over it, which would take tremendous strength, or she will have to go to the right, which is more sheer. There are usually holes and bolts left by other climbers, though I couldn't see any through my binoculars." He shook his head. "Incredible."

Madina reached the halfway mark. A gust of wind popped Ajay in the face, making him blink. The clouds, which had meandered across the sky all morning, now moved faster. Dust rose in little serpents.

"It looks like a bit of wind is coming," the German said. Then under his breath he added, "No rope, no harness, no biners, no anchors, no water—"

"Shut up," Ajay said.

The German looked sideways at Ajay. "I am sorry." He moved off to a small group of climbers and talked. They turned their faces to Ajay and then Madina, who climbed on. The wind pulled at Ajay's hair.

"Bullies," he murmured. He strode back to the German's car and grabbed the drum bag from the back seat. Ajay walked fast across the field toward the rock wall. Five meters from the base, he sat cross-legged and arranged his drums. He set his eyes on Madina and played.

Madina looked down at him. She smiled, or at least he thought she did.

"That's right," he said to the rising wind that grabbed at his hair, his clothes. "You go ahead and blow. You'll have to blow yourself out to beat her." And he made the sliding sound on his drum, the one Madina liked for the heaviness. *Da-loop*. Like a single drop of water falling from a spout.

Ta-ta-te-ray-kay te-te-ta-kah, he played, hands moving faster and harder. From which she might gain strength. On which she could focus the power in her muscles and fingers and mind.

"Rise," Ajay half-sang to the rhythm of his drums. "You go where I can't. Where none of us can. And when you get there, spit at that wind for me. Laugh, too. Laugh now, and when you get to the bottom, I'll laugh with you."

He and Madina would laugh. *Tum-te-te-tum-tum. Te-ray- te-kay.*

Ajay's neck muscles ached in rhythm with his drums from

163

watching Madina climb and from the risk, too, of her diving headlong into the hard ground before him. When she neared the bulge of rock – the chickenhead – she seemed to search for a way around. She tried to get a grip in one place, then another until her hands lodged. Her feet swung free. Ajay held his breath. Then her feet found purchase again and she pulled herself up and over. She slipped out of sight. Sweat slid down his temple to the corner of his eye. He jumped to his feet to see if she'd made the top.

The German joined Ajay. Then the other climbers did, too. They swore and whispered. The excited murmur of something big about to happen, but not to them. Something nearby and visual. Ajay concentrated on Madina, though he couldn't see her.

"She's clinging to the rock, just above the chickenhead," said a husky woman with a rounded, muscled back and a pair of binoculars. "She's got a grip with both hands, but not a good one."

"What's she doing?" another climber said.

"Just hanging there. Looking down."

"Go up and get her," Ajay yelled at Felix.

"How could I get to her in time?" the German said. Then he twisted around. "Does anyone have an air mattress?"

"Are you fucking joking?" a tall bearded American said.

"It is better than nothing," the German said.

Three people turned and ran toward their vehicles.

Ajay broke from the group.

"Where are you going?" the German yelled.

When Ajay reached the cliff face, he put a foot on a slim ledge and gripped a wedge of rock. He pulled himself up.

"If you go up then we'll have to save you, too," Felix said. He pulled the back of Ajay's T-shirt, making him fall back to the ground.

Ajay fell on his behind. He sprang to his feet and scoured Felix's blue eyes.

"Don't do that again," Ajay said. Even though he'd done the same thing to Madina that long time ago in the desert. To keep her from the same kind of idiocy.

Felix threw up his hands and stepped back. Ajay turned to the wall and climbed. The stone so close, so suffocating. But without his drums and backpack, he also felt lighter than he'd ever been before.

164

The woman with binoculars gasped. "One of her hands slipped." Everyone talked.

"Here's a mattress."

"How fast can you blow it up?"

"He's coming with another one."

"Like this shit's going to do any good."

Ajay climbed and the voices faded. He kept his eyes on the chickenhead far above, the bulge that blocked his view of Madina. *Dhat tereki.* Then he yelled his damnation.

"*Dhat tereki!*" he said. "You up there, Madina, you crazy woman!" And he pulled, his fingers gripping the cold surface that grew smoother the higher he went.

"You come down, do you hear me?" he yelled, his feet clinging to the rock by a thin overlap of boot and ledge and his legs shook. "*Bakvas!*" he yelled, wind whipping around his head and body. "When I get you, that's it, goddess or no goddess. I'm going to—"

Then the wind died. Just died.

"Madina!"

A gust of wind slammed his body from the right. Ajay fell.

CHAPTER 24

Ajay sat on the ground, leg propped on his backpack and a chemical cold pack over his swollen ankle. The other climbers milled at a distance. Eying him. Shaking their heads.

Ajay looked from one face to the next. He looked down and yanked a yellow wildflower up by the roots. When the voices grew in volume, he looked up. Madina jogged toward him, her eyes on the uneven ground. Leaping lightly around the climbers, who turned to watch her pass, the American calling out, *Fucking amazing*. She neared, slowed and finally knelt before him. She sat back on her heels, hands on her thighs. Her top, pants, hands and bridge of her nose streaked with gray dust. The wind playing with the ends of her hair. So docile now.

"At least it wasn't a belly flop," Ajay said.

Madina smiled.

"Not good news, I take it."

Madina glanced at the top of the cliff behind him. "Just an old Protector Wind," she said. "It said this place is sacred and I shouldn't be climbing here. None of us should. But then...." She considered the cliff again.

"Yes?"

"A Brother Wind came."

"You never told me about any Brother Winds," Ajay said.

"I didn't know there were any." The clouds uncovered the sun. The western light cut sideways across her eyes, making them almost transparent.

"Well what did our good brother say?"

"To go north," and she gave him a name.

"What's that?"

"A city."

"A big city?"

"I don't know."

"Where?"

"Farther up the coast."

Madina licked her thumb and leaned forward. She wiped blood from Ajay's scraped chin. She stared at the wound with that familiar intensity of a woman trying to make sense of the nonsensical.

"I," she said, "I didn't know you'd fallen, or I would have—"

"Come closer," Ajay whispered.

She leaned closer. Until he could see the rock dust in the crook of her nose. The color gray, like the waves of sea deep within her green eyes, which fluttered over his face before landing on his eyes. Where they focused.

"Is this city it?" Ajay asked. "The place where the war of winds is supposed to start?"

"That's what the wind said."

"But you don't believe our dear brother."

"It's just – strange."

"Why?"

Madina squinted at him. Like he was far away. "Because he gave me an address."

"A street address?"

"Yes."

His head ached. His ankle throbbed. He felt nauseous. Yet he smiled. Because really, how funny.

"So this final storm won't take place out in the open or on the highest mountain in the world," he said. "Or on the loneliest island in the ocean, or in the middle of the sea, or in the center of the biggest city in the world. No, no, this catastrophe will arrive at a certain address in a nothing South American city." Ajay laughed, the amusement worth the pain of having his knocked head grow to five times its normal size. After all he and Madina had been through, only to be invited to the cheap, poorly attended red carpet debut of a second-rate actor. Even Madina smiled, though uncertainly. Apparently thinking twice about what this brother wind had said. Whether the address really existed or not.

But Ajay said nothing. They would go to this city. If the address didn't exist, she would conclude the brother wind had lied and continue onward. But if, by some curious chance, they did find the address, they would go there and wait. And wait. For something to happen. But nothing would happen. Instead of a great war of winds, the wind would blow as usual, the sun would shine and sometimes clouds would cross the sky and sometimes the blue would remain unfettered. Waves would wash up onto the beach and people would go about their business. And though Madina would wait longer than anyone — months, years? — nothing would happen for a long enough period that she'd have to understand there would be no war. Without a war, she'd have to accept peace.

He smiled.

Madina smoothed Ajay's torn T-shirt over his chest, her hand light against him. She pulled the bottom down over his exposed abdomen. She sat back on her heels again.

"There are supposed to be white beaches there," she said.

"Where?"

"On the way."

"White beaches?"

"The winds are trying to kill you."

"So you've said."

"The waterfall. The ship. Here."

"They can't. Not with you around."

She licked her lips. "But maybe we were wrong. Maybe they're trying to kill you because I'm not the one who's supposed to stop the war. Maybe you are."

CHAPTER 25

Madina and Ajay made their way up the coast. They took buses when they could afford them and hitched rides when offered. Most of the way, though, they walked, as they'd done all day and into this night. Now they'd come to the end of a road that just ahead dissolved into a beach that glowed white-blue in the shine of a full moon. Ajay glanced right and left. No houses, no people. A stretch of aloneness.

Madina slipped off her sandals and waited for Ajay to pull off his boots. Madina smiled, eyes luminous. He and she stepped into the sand. She sighed, the sound blending with that of the night's breeze. They walked toward the water and stopped where the small waves curled and collapsed into sheets of water that rushed up the sand, bubbles of air popping and hissing as the water slid back. Clouds stretched across the sky, thin rags of silk. The breeze blew the palm fronds high overhead, the sound a whisper.

"What wind is watching us now?" Ajay asked.

Madina arched her neck to study the treetops against the starred sky. Ajay kept his eyes on her, the rhythm of the small waves around his feet coursing through his body.

"I don't know," Madina said. "It's like a tickle in my ear."

"A tickle."

"Yes. Now it's humming a tune, something slow."

171

Ajay stepped before Madina. She kept her gaze on the sky, head tilted back and to the right. Her throat exposed. His eyes slid from her face, past her shoulders and waist, down her legs to the bells. He fell to his knees and placed his hand on the anklet, his fingers curling around her ankle, the metal of her anklet cool against her warm skin. Madina shivered. Still she didn't look at him, yet she didn't draw away, either.

"A breeze of laziness," she said.

Ajay rode his hands up over the curve of her calves.

"It runs in and out of the palms all day, waiting to play," Madina said, her breath stopping, starting.

Ajay buried his face in her skirt. He rested his cheek against her pelvis and inhaled her scent. He entwined his fingers in the fabric, then pulled down. Her skirt lowering. Over her thighs, her knees, to her ankles. He bent low and kissed her ankles. He rose to his knees and smoothed a hand around the back of her thigh, his fingers curling between her legs. He kissed her other thigh, his tongue an upward stroke tasting of her salt. His hands curved over her hips and his tongue found the shallow of her bellybutton. A worn shell. A tiny cup. His hands circled her ribcage and pushed upward, lifting the fabric of her blouse. Ajay trembled. Starved, yet unsure. That she could, that she would, after an enslaved youth.

But then he felt her hand on his head, her fingers through his hair. Doubt bled. Weariness fled. So that he didn't know her except for what his lips touched, and there within the darkness of his closed eyes, he learned her anew. Though not until his mouth met hers did he understand. What he could only know after the long walk, the long ride. After the ocean storm and nights of sleeping on floors and buying and wearing of gifts. That after being scarred, broken, walked away from and left, that this swirl of air between them — this merging of breath — was their music.

Their sweat ran in a pool of humid night air; this mentally and physically scarred woman and this thief, now freed from the prison of their lives, sins forgiven, the entrance to a new life here, at the end of the road. The new life a string of moments like this one on a white sand beach under shredded clouds and a starred sky, making music for a yellow moon, for each other.

Where before, Ajay had been an observer, a wanderer, a passerby, he was now the reason for her loose, fluid motion. The foundation she grasped and on which she shifted her weight. Gripping his shoulder. Raking his skin with her fingernails. He suctioned his lips to her salty flesh. Feeling how she wanted to release, to fall, but he wouldn't let her. So she kept on, closer to the top, and still Ajay didn't let go. He claimed her hands for his own, shut his eyes, grit his teeth. He pushed her over the top and breathless, followed. Though this time — instead of the waterfall, the cliff — instead of fighting, he let go, eyes closed, body free.

He landed on his back, panting, the black beads resting against his throat. Madina leaned over him. He could tell by the particles of sand that fell from her hair onto his cheek.

"Will you be all right?" she whispered.

"No." But he smiled.

CHAPTER 26

Madina opened her eyes. She lay on her side facing the window of this hotel room on the outskirts of the city, far from the tourist beaches and expensive shops. She watched a fly walk up the light blue curtains that waved in the morning breeze. The fly stopped, climbed higher, then buzzed away. Madina put a hand on her bare stomach. She yawned and stretched her arm upward toward the slow-turning ceiling fan. She rolled onto her back and looked at the left side of the bed. Empty.

Madina rolled her tongue over her teeth and turned her gaze to the fan, then to the jagged crack on the ceiling. Someone in another room turned on a radio and fast music played. Low voices spoke muffled words. Heavy footsteps sounded outside in the hall, making the wood floorboards creak. The footsteps pounded down the stairs to the lobby.

A scratched painting in a dented wooden frame hung on the wall. The picture showed the back of a boy walking down a road with a fishing pole over his shoulder, his dog following.

"Chirayu," she whispered. The new name he'd chosen for himself. Though he wouldn't tell her its meaning. He only smiled. Him and his jokes. She smiled too, now. Yet, as she stared at the painting, her smile faded. Because the boy was walking away.

She sat up and saw his drums on their cloth rings where he'd set them last night on the chipped wood dresser. The round drum with the dented silver hull tilted right, toward the window. The other drum, slim and made of dark wood, tilted left toward the door. The

175

tops of both were covered by their little ruffled green and orange caps, now faded and ragged at the edges.

His drums. "Your heart." A whisper.

Madina touched her fingertips to her lower lip. Her eyes skated to the closed door, back to the drums then to the painting of the little boy, his back to her. Walking away. Sweat formed on her forehead and goose bumps on her arms. She listened. Several breezes mingled and murmured, the sound like that of people talking in another room, people who didn't want to be heard. There was muted laughter. A secret joke.

Madina slid out of bed and stood, naked. Again she cocked her ear. A bicycle clattered by two stories below her open window. The voices of the winds lowered to a whisper. She put on her blouse and her skirt. When a breeze slipped through the window and flared the fabric, Madina slammed her heel on the floor. Her skirt deflated. *Him.* She whipped her head to where the sound had come from, in the street.

Yesterday, she and Ajay had gotten a city map that showed the street and the address that had been given to her by the Brother Wind. They had agreed they would go there today. She glanced to the small desk where they had left the map before going to sleep. It was gone. But he'd showed her the map the night before and used a finger to trace the route. 'This way,' he said.

Madina squatted and set the green canvas bag on the floor. She widened the opening and set the silver-bottomed drum inside. She added the smaller, heavier drum and zipped the bag closed. She put on his backpack and scooped up her pouch then lifted the drum bag and unlocked the door. Madina stopped in the small lobby and glanced out the torn screen door to the street beyond. A squat, broad-shouldered black woman sat behind the desk, shelling nuts and popping them into her mouth.

"Did you—" Madina said in English.

The woman looked up. "Ay?"

"Did you," Madina said, "see a man come through—"

The woman swiped a hand as people did when swatting at flies. She mumbled something in Portuguese and turned her attention to the nuts in her hand. Then she seemed to remember something, and as Madina was beginning to walk away called out to her. When

Madina turned, she was waving a paper at her. A note Ajay had left her.

Madina took the note. On one side were handwritten strokes, while on the other, small printed symbols. Judging by the ragged edge on one side, the paper had been torn from a book.

Madina held out the paper. "You read to me?" she said in English.

The woman blinked. She shook her head. "No English."

Madina folded the paper and slipped the square into her pouch. "*Shukran*," she murmured, and repeated her thanks in English. But the woman didn't look up. Madina hurried out the door.

The hotel was located on a street of dilapidated buildings and stores. Madina turned in a circle until the wind blew full in her face. North. *Yes*. She followed.

Ajay walked fast and stayed close to the crumbling buildings made of stucco and plywood and in some cases, corrugated metal. He kept his eyes moving while scanning everything around him. The farther he went, the fewer people he saw. Many of the shabby buildings were vacant. How easy peril could spring from emptiness and ruin. Then again, the danger would be nothing he couldn't handle.

Judging by the neighborhood, the address, if it existed, probably belonged to an empty building of broken windows. If the area was safe, he'd bring her back to see for herself. Then she could wait, as long as she wanted, for something to happen. When nothing did, she'd have to wake up. Once she was freed, they'd both be freed. He shivered, the enormity of riches at hand.

Ajay walked, now and then tapping a rhythm on his thighs with his fingers. He missed the familiar weight of his drums, but knew they were safe with Madina. He would take care of this errand quickly and be back at the hotel soon enough. He passed two old women and a husky man riding a small bike. The neighborhood continued to deteriorate. Shattered windows, boarded doors, collapsed roofs, weeds of tree height, their odor thick and sour. His shoulder muscles tightened. His legs readied to run. His fingers drummed faster on his thighs.

He squinted at a faded number on a building. Not the right

one, but he was getting closer. He was glad he'd left his drums. He was glad, too, he'd left a note for Madina, one shocking enough to stop her from following. Better she read the note and suffer from the anxiety for awhile. Then when he got back, he'd apologize and tell her what he had found. Ajay had always assumed that if Madina could speak English, she could read it, too.

Movement. A man passed. A man half a meter taller than Ajay and older by a few decades. The man walked with stooped shoulders, the posture of men with no hopes or cares. He kept his eyes straight ahead.

Ajay didn't alter his pace until he passed the man. Then Ajay slowed and glanced over his shoulder. The man was gone.

Ajay jogged down the empty street to the next alley and walked the full length while glancing back every few seconds. When he reached the end, he peered around the corner, this street deserted, too, though narrower than the one he'd been on. A serpentine crack ran down the middle of the packed earth. A skinny gray dog with long, flapping ears trotted toward him in a sideways gait; a dog so skinny and perpetually hungry that it had long ago lost the canine propensity to bark, much less wag its tail or bite.

Ajay stepped into the street and walked. He stuck close to the buildings and noted alleys and routes of escape while scanning for motion. And how strange to be without the weight of his drums. How light. A tingle crept up his neck, but he didn't stop. He couldn't stop now, and wouldn't. She needed to know, to see.

He walked so close to the building that his left shoulder brushed a board, a window, a doorpost. He saw an alley ahead and stepped away into the open street, in case anyone should be waiting in the alley. And there was someone waiting. A boy. The two stared at one another, the boy tall as Ajay, but younger by two, maybe three years. A brown-skinned boy, thin of shoulder, wild of hair. He wore a dingy white shirt that billowed open in the breeze, showing his concave chest. The boy smiled.

Madina walked down the middle of the street, her eyes searching faces and shops. She passed a bakery on her left. A door opened and banged shut, the scent of bread heavy, then brushed away by a slight breeze.

Soon she was walking over graveled dirt beneath trees that looked like they'd grown back after being badly hacked. She continued, vacant buildings on the right and a stream of green slime on the left.

After two blocks she made a left down a narrow side street and stopped behind a half-collapsed shanty. She set the drum bag on the ground and untied her pouch. She slid the note under the horn – the horn she'd refrained from throwing into the ocean after her talk with Henry Dawson on the ship. The horn that could bring a quick and merciful death to humanity instead of a prolonged period of suffering and starvation. Then she pulled out her knife. She set the blade on the ground, lodged the pouch in a pile of weeds and covered the bundle with rocks. She picked up the drum bag with her left hand and the knife with her right, the blade pointed down and hidden in the folds of her skirt.

Madina cut back to the main road. She stopped and listened to the silence. The wind had disappeared.

After the boy in the alley, Ajay turned the first corner he came to and jogged. He took another right then a left and another left until the address he sought was a block away, or should be. Because no grinning punk would keep Ajay away. He'd see. He'd leave. He'd bring her back, and with an armed guard, if necessary.

Ajay circled the location. No smiling boy. The streets slanted down here, toward the ocean, and the buildings — what was left of them — were interspersed with weedy lots backed by scraggly, densely-packed trees. Ajay glanced at the sun to keep track of his direction. He made one turn, then another. He glanced behind him, the movement so small and fast he almost missed the image, of someone's heel disappearing around a corner.

"*Bakvas,*" Ajay said under his breath. Running now, he rounded a corner to see a heavy-set black man step out of a doorway ahead. He faced Ajay. There was no attempt to pretend friendliness or disinterest.

Ajay dodged down an alley only wide as his shoulders. Another man blocked the end of the alley. Ajay jumped and grabbed the edge of the building's low, flat roof. He swung himself up and ran along the rooftop so decayed his feet sunk a little with each

179

stride. When the roof ended he jumped a couple meters to the next roof, his strides clattering on the metal.

He heard a shout on his left followed by a higher-pitched shout on his right. He ran to the corner of the building. Far down the street the heavy-set man and another man ran toward him. Ajay jumped to the ground and ran the length of an alley, only to stumble on rubble and tumble out into a street in front of three males coming from the left. Ajay rolled to his feet and ran the other way, no longer sure of his direction. Two of the men ran into the street ahead of Ajay and he halted. His only escape was to pass them, so he waited until they drew close, then sprinted through the widest divide. But one of them caught Ajay by the back of his T-shirt. The material ripped and Ajay fell. He jumped to his feet, but a hand grabbed the back of his pants and pulled him around with such force he fell on his behind. He snapped his eyes from one face to another. Surrounded by four men and the boy, all of them common, dirty, street-crawling thieves like himself. Again Ajay jumped to his feet where he remained crouched and ready to spring.

Then Ajay glanced up and in faded blue paint, saw the street number he'd been looking for. His mouth dropped open and though sweat ran into his eyes, he blinked away the sting and stood straight. He smiled, then laughed, his laughter growing by the moment.

The building where the war of winds was supposed to begin had a flaking, black-painted door where customers once entered beside a wide metal roll-up door for vehicles. Painted above the doors was a now-faded red cartoon car wearing a smile between two headlight eyes. Though surrounded by men who didn't seem to have any sense of humor, Ajay's smile remained.

"An abandoned auto body shop," he said and shook his head. Then he turned in a circle, taking his time to study the faces of the street dogs. Animals that would no doubt eat each other if necessary. Thugs risen from the layered grit on which they were born, making them Ajay's Brazilian brothers. Of the four men, one had a stocky build with black chest hair frothing over the scooped neck of his dirty white T-shirt. Next to him stood the tall, skinny man with the stooped shoulders and no apparent cares. The third man was the black, with muscular torso and short legs. A goiter bulged from the neck of the fourth man.

And who could forget the boy. Of the five, only he smiled. And what a charming smile, too. One that implied Ajay was too stupid to understand what lay beneath the grin.

Ajay kept his eyes on the boy while addressing the sky. "Are you there, wind? If so, now would be a good time to start your war."

The men looked at one another. Ajay laughed. The punch came from behind and landed on the back of his neck. Ajay fell to his hands and knees. He shook his head, bubbles of white floating in his vision. He spit into the dirt and a fine thread of saliva stretched between his mouth and the ground in a straight line that proved the wind had disappeared. And how funny, that the wind should plague him in one way or another for weeks — pushing, pulling, whipping, drowning — only to abandon him when he most needed a storm.

"Such a warrior," Ajay murmured.

A hand grabbed Ajay under the armpit, pulled him to his feet and shoved him forward with a fist between his shoulder blades. Maybe he could angle right and break through their line. But his neck had turned into two knives, their blades grating against one another, and the white dots before his eyes had turned to red.

"I have nothing," Ajay said in English because he didn't know enough Portuguese yet. They ignored him and pushed him toward the building's door. He could sense their need to hurt him, the activity an amusement on a dull day. How disappointed they'd be to learn he had nothing of value, the reason the laughter remained in his chest. Because he'd been smart. He'd left his treasure behind. His drums, and Madina.

A hand pushed Ajay from behind and he stumbled through the black door. "Thanks for getting me off the deserted street," Ajay said. A careless tone, yet he had trouble swallowing. "It's dangerous out there."

Inside the building, half the ceiling had collapsed, the remnants in a heap in the far right corner of the two-story room. The door through which he'd come seemed the only obvious escape, other than a broken window on the back wall near a small, round table and several chairs. Only a few glass shards remained stuck in the window frame. One jump and he'd be through. Though Ajay didn't allow his eyes to rest on the window, the boy seemed to sense the possibility and sat on the ledge. He smiled. He lifted a hand and worked a piece of glass back and forth, a lackluster attempt to dislodge the shard from the window frame.

"There are only four chairs," Ajay said to the four men who surrounded him. "I suppose someone will have to stand."

The men didn't say anything. What did they expect? He was a musician, not a comic. Then again, he was a thief, too, and knew how this worked. He considered his stained T-shirt, his worn pants. He slid his hands into his pockets, pinched the ends and pulled them out. He looked at the empty lining of his pockets, one of which had a hole.

"See? Nothing," Ajay said.

The men shifted on their feet and looked at one another. They didn't look too smart, so Ajay lifted his torn T-shirt and turned in a circle, showing them his ribs. He lowered his shirt and considered his boots, which had taken him through the sand to Madina. Ajay squatted, unlaced the boots and took them off. He threw them at the two men in front of him. They jumped back. The boots landed with a *thunk* that echoed off the cracked concrete walls. The man with the long torso stepped from behind Ajay and grabbed the boots, then disappeared again.

Again a slight move, one Ajay barely caught, of how the boy glanced at Ajay's throat. Ajay put a hand to the black bead necklace. Remembering the occasion when Madina stood before him and with a solemn expression, lowered the beads into his palm, he felt a deep sorrow at what he was about to do.

He fingered the beads, his eyes moving from face to face until they rested on the smiling boy. Ajay gripped the beads. Then he smiled, too, and yanked. The necklace broke and the round balls rained on the floor in a sputtering clatter as the beads bounced and scattered. The men jumped back and watched, their shoulders, hands, necks tense, like Ajay had opened a cage of scorpions that scurried in every direction. Only when the last bead stopped rolling — so many black, dead beetles — did the men look at him. Ajay returned his gaze to the boy and the two stared at one another. Though the boy's eyes narrowed, his smile remained. He worked the jagged piece of glass back and forth, back and forth.

"Now it's time to beat me so I can go," Ajay said.

The boy nodded, though Ajay knew the kid didn't know any English, just as Ajay knew the boy didn't have any aspirations, much less the stamina to reach them. He was a mistake — one of humanity's many — who didn't go anywhere or learn anything.

A hand from behind shoved Ajay toward the small table. The men in front of him parted to let him pass. A hand spun Ajay and he fell onto a chair. The tall skinny man produced a liquor bottle of brown glass and unscrewed the cap. He held out the drink.

Ajay didn't need to look behind him to know that this time he'd literally been backed into a corner, with no way out. That these animals didn't just intend to beat him, but meant to kill him. Yet the corners of his mouth turned up, because his time with her — his risk for her — had not been without payment. The bigger his smile grew, the faster the tension flowed from his body, leaving him loose, his mind filled with images of her. Of his payment, and in his mind he saw the first finger rays of the rising sun.

"Ah," Ajay said, because every moment the dawn grew brighter, lifted higher until he saw the entirety of the splendor. A vision he'd had to wait for until this very moment to witness. He was going to die, but he had found a room of gold in Madina where he would continue to live.

The note. Ajay laughed mirthlessly to himself. Then he laughed out loud into the animal eyes that surrounded him. Because, how funny that he'd written her a note in which he'd exaggerated the danger involved in his sally to find the address. The note had had a double purpose: to keep Madina safe from any danger, and to avoid having to bring his drums with him. A thought that would now serve as a last joke on him. Now Madina would inherit his drums — his heart — whether she wanted to or not.

The edges of the room blurred, then the men did, too, because Ajay couldn't keep his eyes from her. A breeze brushed his cheek, like a kiss, the kiss she'd given him last night, her lips against his skin, so light.

Ajay turned his face toward the breeze. He stared past the darkness of the boy and through the broken window. Eyes far beyond to what the men couldn't see. Ajay inhaled, the air smelling of sand and warm rock. "Have you really turned into a wind, Madina?" he whispered. The air moved over him, around him. His smile deepened. "Yes? Then take me with you."

When Madina lifted her eyes from the road, she stopped. Four men and a boy walked toward her, their eyes down and mouths laughing. Yet by the time Madina glanced at the alley she'd just passed and back again, the five had spotted her and stopped, no longer laughing. Only the boy continued to smile, eyes surprised in a pleased way. She dropped her eyes to his blood-splattered shirt. When she lifted them to his face, he smiled wider. Madina gripped the knife hidden behind a fold in her skirt.

A man with hairy shoulders sauntered toward her and she stepped back. The hairy man stopped and the others laughed. Two of them split off to either side and danced their way behind her with jokey hands and faces until they encircled her. They whistled and called to her in their language, their voices sharp and clear in the still air. Her eyes cooled. Her lips a thin ledge of stone.

Madina turned in a slow circle. Someone pinched her in the behind. She jumped and although fast to turn, missed the boy, who hopped out of reach and laughed, the men laughing, too. The black man swaggered forth and tried to grab her wrist, but Madina swung Ajay's drum bag and nearly hit him in the head. He fell back on his hands. The others laughed more.

The hairy man came from behind and circled his arm around her waist. She stabbed him in the thickest part of his forearm and he cried out and pulled away. The others closed in, no longer laughing. Madina crouched and spun one way then the other, the knife outstretched. The black man caught the handle of the drum bag, but Madina pulled hard, drawing him close. She swung the knife in a swift straight thrust, and he stumbled away, hunched over and clutching his abdomen.

Someone slammed into her from behind. She fell on her chest. The attacker sat on her back. She threw her weight to the side and rolled him off and saw he was the thin man. She flipped over and kicked him in the throat with her heel and he fell back. She jumped to her feet, recovering the drum bag.

Madina opened her mouth and yelled a single note that grew louder and louder. When she ran out of breath, she inhaled and yelled again. She hit the thin man in the stomach with the drum bag. She sliced the boy across his forehead. He staggered away, with his hand clutching the wound, blood streaming between his fingers. No longer smiling. She stabbed the man with the goiter and he grunted and fell to his knees.

The hairy man, bleeding heavily from his arm, pulled her by the hair and instead of resisting, she moved toward him, shoving her head into his stomach. He sat on the ground with a thud. She grabbed the metal-bottomed drum that rolled out of the torn bag and raised the instrument with both hands. She brought the hull down on his head over and over until he was still.

She stood, panting, and staggered in a full circle. The hairy man lay still. The black man was some distance away, walking slowly off as he clutched his abdomen. The man with the goiter was still on his knees, his arms across his stomach. The thin man and boy were gone. And still the tree fronds didn't move. Her legs collapsed and she sat in the dirt. Her lips and scalp bled. Her blouse was torn down the side and her skirt was splattered with blood. The street remained empty.

Madina swallowed and rolled to all fours. Blood from her face fell to the hard-packed dirt, each drop a black, dust-covered bead. She pushed herself up and stood, wavering. She raised her left hand and stared at the two middle fingers that were no longer straight, but rather bent to the side. She lowered her hand.

Her eyes wandered and stopped on the hilt of her knife, the blade gone. Her eyes wandered again and stopped again, this time on the metal-hulled drum. She took a step forward, limping on her right leg, and picked up the drum, its bottom crushed and covered with bits of hair, skin, blood. She cradled the drum in her left arm and with her fingertips, brushed the dirt from the goatskin head, now split down the middle. She raised the drum to her trembling lips and blew. Little grains of dirt skittered across the surface and fell through the dark hole.

Madina limped to the torn green bag, then to the smaller drum. Four lashings broken and three wooden pegs missing. She licked her lips and winced, her breath shallow. She set the drums together and tied the bag closed. Then she stood, the drum bag in one hand. She stared at the building before her, at the faded, cartoon-like painting of a little red car wearing a smile between its two headlight eyes. She hobbled through the black door.

She gazed upon Ajay, who lay on his back, his eyes open to the ceiling and arms thrown wide, a black blanket of blood spread beneath him. Flies buzzed and crept about his mouth and ears.

A glass shard stuck out of Ajay's neck, the broken remnant smeared with dirt. Madina's eyes slipped down his body to the insides of his trouser pockets, which were white, and his feet, which were bare. The black beads of his necklace rubbled the broken floor of gray cement.

Her eyes crept back to his open eyes. She lifted the drum bag a little.

"They're a little damaged, is all," she said. "I'll get them fixed for you."

Part III

Ana fahhem.

I understand.

CHAPTER 27
Jamaica

The young woman had been told that this place rented rooms at very moderate rates. That the owner of this house was an obeah woman, who knew things about people they didn't know about themselves. Things about what they should do and where they should go when they no longer had any idea about either. So she had trudged wearily up the dirt track to the door of the large yellow, green and blue house among the lush trees and bushes on a hillside overlooking the ocean. She wore a tattered skirt, faded and stained, and a blouse that had been torn and crudely repaired with ill stitches of fishing line. She carried a two-lump sack of faded green canvas under one arm, and in the crook of the other, a dirty pouch.

The door opened. A small black girl stared up at the young woman without smiling. The girl's black eyes wandered over the woman's garb, then returned to her face and studied the scar. The girl turned and ran down the hall, soon swallowed by the interior darkness. A time passed in which the wind made the tree branches and fern fronds sway overhead and made the red flowers of an enormous poinsettia plant fold and unfold. The outline of a taller person approached, rocking side to side, foot to foot. The door opened wider and an old black woman appeared dressed in a shapeless, red dress of white flowers. The colors bright. Excruciating. The young woman lowered her eyes to the old woman's bowed legs and the crooked toes shod in white flip-flops.

189

"Are you looking for a room?" the old woman asked, her voice a low rumble of English.

The young woman nodded.

"You have Jamaican money?" the old woman asked.

The young woman nodded again.

"You're going to have to take a shower before you occupy your room, the old woman said, though not unkindly."

The young woman said nothing.

"I'm Verde," the old woman said. "You got a name?"

The young woman nodded. "Madina," she said.

"You got a last name?" the old woman asked.

Madina was silent. Verde sighed. "Well, the police don't bother me much about names. You can stay the night. I won't charge you."

Madina's eyes fluttered open. She stared at the ceiling, the moon through the window above her head offering a drift of light. Its beams bounding from one wall of the small room to another, the wind thrashing the trees outside. Madina's breathing accelerated by the moment. She shivered beneath her sheet. She strained to listen. But the winds roared and whined, sputtered and barked, punched and stroked all at once.

She waited, her breath a pant. She moved her shaking body to the edge of the narrow bed and lowered an arm. Her fingers touched the floor and she felt around, then more frantically until her hand touched the bag. The drums. Her hand moved to the pouch and squeezed. She pulled her hand back under the sheet and closed her eyes.

Still the wind's intensity increased. Body-sized fists slammed into the walls, making the house shake. Air wailed through the trees, the wind rushing, slapping, hissing, spitting. She kept her eyes closed, her body a rock.

The wind lashed the wind chimes and raked the trees with a murderous hand. Beat them against the house, turning branches into woody claws that scraped the roof above her. As if trying to get in. Madina remained still. The darkness roared louder. The wind whistled through cracks, whined around corners, tore at the roof. The wind threw missiles against the wall. A broom. a flowerpot.

Then amid the riot, the fury, came a whisper. How could she hear a whisper amid the riot, the whirling? Yet she did. She looked up, the sound creeping on the roof above her head, that of dried leaves skittering to the right, then the left.

Scritch scratch.

A current of air thin and quiet, seemingly of no consequence. A wind that seemed to sniff, using long, string fingers to crawl, to explore. Searching for cracks to enter. The woman trembled. Her lips, her arms, her legs.

A blast of air threw the leaves off the roof. Madina gripped the bed and gasped, her eyes running right and left. The wind thrashed, the air laden with the smell of damp wood.

Then the shutter on the window above her head trembled, like fingers pressing inward. Pressing downward one slat at a time. Madina didn't move, her unblinking eyes on the ceiling. With a sigh, a breeze slipped beneath the last slot, the first touch a caress on her forehead. The breeze swooped down between her eyebrows and brushed beneath her nose. She inhaled, the smell of the night's perfume. Of insects, wet earth, flowers asleep on their stems.

The breeze welled in the crevice of her lips like rainwater, a pool that filled and spilled over into the notch of her throat. From there the breeze crept over her breasts and hovered before flowing over the rest of her body. The air crept between her legs and stretched out along her thighs.

Her eyes flew open. Paralyzed, as what remained of her spirit drained away. The Lulling Breeze took its time, lingering over her chest, her belly. Then the snake of current slipped over her toes, and was gone.

Madina was still lying on her back in the small room when the light of dawn crept out of the east, spilling over the window sill and onto the floor. The tinkle of shells and the ring of metal from the wind chimes that hung from the eaves outside the windows were silent now, after their riotous sounds during the wind storm last night. She listened, almost fearfully, for the sounds that would come to her ears with the approach of day. Footsteps. The sound of a side-to-side hobble that stopped just outside the door.

"I won't need you anymore today, Renee," Verde said in a low voice. "Go on home now. I'll see you Monday."

The girl spoke, her words an unheard whisper.

"I think so, too," Verde said, "but that's why they come to me, some of them. It's nothing I can't handle. You go on."

She knocked lightly on the door and then came into the room. "You can come out and have some breakfast any time you want," Verde said. "As long as it's not after nine o'clock."

Madina, sitting up on the bed now, nodded her head. She turned her green eyes upon the old woman, groping for the words in English she wanted to say. "Someone told me you could answer some questions I have, about the wind."

Verde stared steadily at her in silence for a moment. Insects hummed. The fern tips outside the window twisted and waved. The chimes clicked and swayed. *Tinkle clink-clink.* The wind began to increase.

A hummingbird had been fluttering at the feeder hanging along the roof edge, the wings moving so fast they were no more than shadows. Now it zipped off without finishing its drink. The clouds coming off the sea sailed large and fast, the thick of them tinged with dark gray.

"People come to me because they got problems," Verde said. "They don't think I can tell what's bothering them. All they know is they go away feeling better. But I can feel it, the little pockets of trouble they hide. From other people. From themselves. But you..." Verde shook her head. "You're a mass of torment whipped into a storm ready to burst. I've lived here almost twenty years now, seen all kinds of hurricanes, but I've never seen anything like it. Like you got ghosts swirling all around you. *Mm-mm.* What kind of catastrophe is it you're holding on to?"

Madina lifted her eyes to Verde, who sucked in a breath, hand to her heart.

Madina ate in Verde's kitchen, an arm around her bundle and the beaten green bag at her feet. Strands of her tangled hair blew in the strong wind coming through the window above the sink.

Verde sat with her old hands folded on the wooden table. She gazed through the open window to the clouds against the darkening sky.

Madina pushed the last bite of bread into her mouth. She chewed slowly with her lips closed.

"That's too bad about your friend," Verde said.

Madina remained silent.

"My son was killed," Verde said. "Only twenty. In the Bronx. You know the Bronx?"

Madina shook her head.

"That's how come I moved here. Get away from all that ugliness. Miles and miles I traveled, and what did I find? That it's here, too. But at least it's farther from my own house, a good walk instead of out in the hallway or in the apartment above."

Verde leaned forward, an elbow on the table. She set her chin in her palm. Madina brushed crumbs from her lips.

"Lord, you look so bone tired," Verde said. "But you would, wouldn't you, traveling all alone month after month, doing this, doing that, looking for this war. Ending up here, because somebody told you I can see things that other people can't."

"Yes," Madina said.

Outside a discordant tapping began, of drops on leaves. Then the rain poured, the sound a steady rush. Soon water streamed off the roof's edge.

Still, Verde watched Madina.

"So you think this wind came last night? Just snuck right in and stole your spirit?" Verde said.

"Yes."

"So now, are you going to blow that horn of yours because you got nothing else to lose?"

Madina remained silent.

Verde rolled her lips together and again shook her head. "The end of the road for you, is it? What is it you think you'll do now?"

When Madina did not answer, Verde said, "When you run out of places to look for your war of the winds you can come back here. I'll make room for you."

CHAPTER 28

After breakfast Verde sat in a white plastic chair on her patio, eyes shut. The enormous, low clouds sliding by overhead. The morning air cool and the ocean gray. Verde yawned, and hearing a sound behind her opened her eyes and looked over her shoulder at Madina, who stood in the doorway leading to the patio. She held a dirty, folded paper between two fingertips of her right hand. The wind tugged at the corners of the note, as if to snatch it away.

"Come over here and sit down," Verde said.

Madina slowly came near but remained standing.

Verde shifted her eyes to the ocean and scratched the loose skin under her chin.

"Some wind we had last night," she said. "Kept me up half the night. Then when it died down, the stillness kept me up the other half." She shook her head. "A wind like that can sure fill a person's mind with dark thoughts. *Mm-hmm.*

"And I think we got another storm coming," she said. "Don't know if it's the one you come to see, though. Not that I'd mind. There's something to that, what you say. The idea of winds scouring the earth, making it clean. A new start for some other kind of life. Something better."

Madina looked down at the note in her hand.

"What would it be like, the winds warring and carrying on?"

Madina said nothing.

"That bad, huh? And you're supposed to stop it." Verde

rested an elbow on the back of her chair. "The thing is, you don't look like you want to."

Madina remained silent.

Verde shook her head. "No spirit left in you, huh?" She gazed at the ocean. "So we're all going to die because you're just too worn out. Because the wind stole your spirit last night. But... I suppose the earth could use a good housecleaning. Life would probably start all over again, but at least it would take us another few million years to figure out how to kill each other for no good reason."

Verde scratched the back of her head, the small gold hoops in her ears jiggling. She pushed out of the chair, took a step and winced.

"Can you read?" Madina said.

"Can I read?" Verde said. "Sure. Why? Can't you?"

Madina said nothing.

Verde pointed at the note. "That from him?"

Madina nodded.

"You want me to read it to you?" Verde said.

"Yes. Please." Madina lifted her arm. Where before the wind tugged at the paper, the air now tore at the note. But Madina hung on.

Verde read, first silently then aloud. She handed back the paper to Madina, who stared at the note. She blinked and looked at the sky of white and gray. Her brows pulled together and her lips began to tremble.

"Ah," she said, the whisper growing to a low moan that stretched out until it almost ended in a cry.

CHAPTER 29

Ajay and Madina's third night in the desert was quiet, save for the *ahhh-ing* of the wind and the sound of his drums. He rolled around in his beat and dropped a note. Rolled around, dropped a beat, a steady rhythm followed by a black hole of silence. He watched Madina as he played, sensing her black was deep, a darkness no one should have to suffer for long. She needed distraction. So Ajay changed the rhythm to something suitable for the story he'd tell her. Something cheerful to augment the atmosphere and emphasize the irony of what he was about to say.

"A little boy goes to a healer," he said, "complaining he's in agony because his heart hurts all the time. 'So take out your heart,' the healer tells him. 'Then I'll die,' the boy says. To which the old man says, 'Then leave it in.'"

Madina looked at Ajay with that intent gaze, the one that made him feel at once needed and yet anxious. Like she consumed what he said, so whatever he said should be worth consuming.

"You mean, there's no choice?" Madina said. "That if something hurts badly, so badly you want to die, you just have to live with it?"

Ajay shrugged.

The tone of Madina's voice dropped, hardened. "That's no choice."

"Untrue," Ajay said. He stopped drumming and lifted a finger before his face. His other hand resting on his drum.

"To live with pain or die," he said. "It's an unfair choice, but it's still a choice."

197

Madina opened her mouth, then clamped her lips shut. She seemed to change before his eyes, in a way so subtle he couldn't describe the transformation. She stretched her neck longer and pressed her shoulders down. Her eyes opened, loosened. She turned her face to the stars. His eyes wandered the line of her neck. They noted the strands of hair that escaped her headscarf, the contrast that of black thread against a white shroud lit by moonlight.

"To escape or stay, that's always the question, no matter the situation," Ajay said. "I myself believe in escape. It's fast, and in most cases, easy, given a little quick thinking. Whereas to stay when there's trouble…" He shook his head. "It's just foolish. Why risk sticking around when it only leads to trouble? That and if you get caught, you lose the ability to make money."

Madina's eyes floated down to his. He smiled. He rose and packed his drums into his bag. He pulled a thin blanket from his backpack and wrapped himself. He turned over and lay with his back to her. He was still for a moment then turned his head to look at her.

"I'm telling you this because you seem like someone who would stay," he said.

He closed his eyes and soon fell asleep.

CHAPTER 30

Madina walked the trail of mud and rock, the Jamaican earth darkened by the mist from the thick, fast-moving clouds that had descended over the mountaintop. She stopped and looked up into the swirling white. No birds flew from the trees. No snakes slithered along the ground. No animals of any kind showed themselves. The trees on either side of the path swayed. The wind made Madina's eyes tear and her hair tangle in a wild flight about her head. She carried the tattered drum bag in her left hand, while in the right she held the note and horn. A blast of wind slammed her from the side, making her stumble to the right. She recovered her balance, her eyes no longer calm.

She cast her eyes skyward briefly, and then turned her face down again. "You like me to tell you things," she told him. "So I will. I'll tell you. "They're all here, Ajay. Can you feel them?" She went on to name them. The Spy Winds, the Land Lovers, the Sweepers and local winds and those from the ocean. All of them scared. A Ground Wind, she said, was in a panic around her ankles, not knowing what to do or where to go. Even the Sister Wind of the island raced around in a fury, not understanding yet.

"'What war of winds,' she keeps asking me. 'No war is going to start here.'"

Madina readjusted her grip on the drum bag and walked on. Monstrous clouds had blocked the sun, turning the afternoon light to dusk.

"Clouds the color of bruises," she said, pointing with the

hand that held the horn. "Dark blue and purple-blue tinged with yellow. The tall clouds like soldiers marching in. They're filling the air with dust and dirt." Madina inhaled. "Of plant life sweet and bitter. And garbage. And salt air. And metal. So many already and it's only the beginning."

Sweat spotted the back of Madina's T-shirt. She passed a broken branch that twirled furiously while tethered to a tree by a strand of bark that would soon break.

"In the beginning," Madina said. She cast her eyes to the ground and recounted. That in the beginning, on the day she met Ajay, her Sister Wind told her to go stop this war.

"But it wasn't my Sister Wind. It was the Lulling Breeze. That killed you. That brought me here and stole my spirit last night." Madina lifted the horn, a precise fit to the curve of her palm. "It wants me to blow the horn. To put an end to it all."

Madina trudged past trees, their trunks black and branches full. Fern fronds thrashed. The path climbed through thick foliage that occasionally fell away to vistas that would have shown her grand views, but were now blocked by clouds. The roiling winds pushed her from both sides so she staggered like a drunk. Her eyes narrowed against the grit flying in the air.

Even now, she said, talking louder now, loud enough to be heard, the two sides were fighting over her. The Pusher Wind pushing her forward, insisting she blow the horn. The local Sister Wind pulling her back, telling her not to listen. That to live and struggle is better than dying.

Madina smiled, the grin bitter. "So that now I have to choose. To do nothing, and prolong suffering."

Or she could blow the horn to summon Aaghat. To erase life. Without life, there would be no more suffering.

So, to live a long and painful existence or die fast and mercifully. "Such an easy choice, if it weren't for you, Ajay."

The wind blew harder. The sky darkened. Madina leaned deeper, her knuckles white from gripping the drum bag and the horn. A ramp of air slid into her, cutting her feet from beneath her. As she fell, her right hand loosened and the horn dropped. Her hand landed on a rock, the note and her palm pierced by a stone. Blood soaked the paper. Madina turned her back to the wind and pushed to a sitting position. She crushed the note in her fist, her eyes darting until she spotted the horn. The wind rolled the instrument downhill, out of reach. She threw her body forward and clamped a hand on the horn. She clutched the instrument to her chest with trembling fingers, the blood from her hand making the horn slippery.

She rolled onto her knees, head into the wind, then got to her feet and picked up the drum bag. She bent forward and took one step and another. She glanced up, squinting at the path to see where it might lead. Thunder cracked behind her shoulder. Another bolt seared the sky and splintered, the needle jags reflecting in her eyes.

Madina yelled now. "Ajay! Do you know what my Sister Wind did before being pushed aside by the Lulling Breeze? She sent you to me. To watch out for me."

Raindrops splattered her face — her nose, her eyelids — then poured. She stuffed the note into the horn and clutched the horn to her body to protect it. The water mixed with the mud on her face and flowed into her eyes. The trees rioted, the sky an injury into which Madina screamed. Of how her Sister Wind must have believed that if Ajay cared for Madina, and she for him, Madina would, if and when necessary, save mankind.

"That I'd have to save mankind in order to save you. But you died!"

Thunder exploded, igniting a tree to her left. Madina dropped into a crouch with hands over her ears, the drum bag and horn at her feet, mouth in a silent scream. Her ears rang and eyes prickled with knife points of glinting light. She unfolded and watched the tree flame despite the rain, the fire a jagged whip.

"You died," she said.

Madina picked up her things, set her shoulder against the wind and continued up the path. One step, two steps, many steps, until the path leveled out and Madina stood atop the mountain in the rain and clouds – before a tree, its thick trunk wrung with branches that led upward into the mist. She tied the horn in a knot of her dirty skirt near the hem. She slung the handle of the drum bag over her shoulder and climbed the ladder of tree branches. The wind drove the rain and clouds through the tree branches, whistling and shrieking. She reached for handholds and footholds on the slippery bark.

Madina climbed until mist swirled below her and above, the

earth gone and sky, too. She stopped and breathing hard, stood on a solid branch, one arm hugging the trunk. A gust of wind hit her from behind and she threw her second arm around the tree, her fingernails digging into the bark. When the gust passed, the clouds opened, offering a glimpse of the island, of the green land and gray ocean.

"You gave me your heart and you died," Madina whispered, the features of her face drawing inward, the lips tightening, the eyebrows crouching, the chin a pinch. The keeper of his heart. "But I can't live anymore."

Rain ran into her mouth. Cut sheets across her vision. Pooled in her eyes. Drowned her ears. She moved just enough to lodge her back against the trunk. She adjusted the drum bag under her left arm and used her fingers to draw up her skirt. Her fingers struggled, but managed to untie the knot. She took the horn in her right hand and the note in her left. She crushed the paper in her fist and raised the horn to her lips.

The rain stopped.

The wind stopped.

Madina stilled.

She blinked, rain dripping from her lashes. Her body shivered as she lowered the horn from her lips. Though the dark clouds hovered, a warm, wet breeze crossed her cheek. She turned her face to the current, closed her eyes and inhaled. She listened, but the breeze was nothing more than a sigh.

"Do you feel it?" she whispered.

Because this wind was not the Lulling Breeze, but rather that which had blown on the desert night when their music first twined. The same wind that whispered on the white sand beach. This was the current Ajay had fought hardest against, but succumbed to, anyway, the mistake of love for which he followed her, and died. Yet before he died, he found his way inside her. A home that now found, he'd never leave. This man who'd wrapped his arms around her with a grip so firm there was no longer a reason for her to hold on. So she let go.

She let go of the Guard Winds. She let go of the Storm Pushers. She let go of the Movers and Jokers and Ghosts. One by one, until she let go of the last, her Sister Wind. She listened for awhile, but they were gone. Madina closed her eyes and inhaled, the air new and sweet, all the voices gone, leaving the world quiet for the first time since she climbed the desert cliff after her mother died. The wind blew, and not many winds, either, but rather only one, a soft current that soughed through tree limbs and leaves.

She opened her eyes, then her palm. She smoothed the damp, crumpled message with her fingertips. The breeze soon dried the blood then lifted the paper beyond her reach. A note she no longer needed, the message forever in her mind.

Madina,

Don't try to follow me. I'm going to meet your winds. If they don't kill me I will be back to tell you about it. If they do kill me, I expect you to stay alive to take care of my drums (as you said you would).

Chirayu
(It means immortal. *Ha-ha.)*

The message dipped once, then twice in a slow downward drift until floating out and away.

Madina looked at the horn in her right hand, staring at it for a long moment, as if it were something she had never seen before. Then she drew back her arm and flung the instrument after the vanished note.

"*Ana fahhem,*" she murmured. *I understand.*

THE END

203

Other Alondra Press Books

Rio San Pedro, by Henry Hollenbaugh
The author's memoirs of his life as a crocodile hunter in Central America in the 1950s. Jonathan Galassi, of Farrar, Straus & Giroux says, "There is a wonderful sense of presence in this novel."

The Canyon Chronicles, by K. Gray Jones
A historical novel of Utah and the conflicts between Mormons and Gentiles during the epoch from the mid 1850's to the early part of the 20th century. A novel that is "sure to please some and infuriate many others."

Nessus The Centaur, by Henry Hollenbaugh
A modern retelling of the ancient myth of Hercules, Dejanira and Nessus the Centaur, in which Hercules is the brutal, surly villain, and Nessus, usually dealt with as a cunning, deceitful rascal, is the tragic hero.

Island Journeys, by Patti. M. Marxsen
Take a lyrical journey with this author across time and across seven islands with a common thread of French history

The Other face of Murder, by Gil Porat
An outstanding first novel by a doctor-writer, dealing with a mysterious murder among friends. Dr. Gil Porat joins the ranks of other medical professionals who have made writing their second love after medicine.

Rhyme of the Fall of Berlin, by Henry Hollenbaugh
A powerful mock-epic poem of World War II, encompassing the birth of Adolph Hitler, the French defeat, the invasion of Russia, Stalingrad, the fall of Berlin, and the death of Hitler and Eva Braun. Written in eight-line rhyming stanzas, sometimes as a parody of poets going from Homer to Dante, to Milton, Shakespeare, Keats, Byron, and others.

Visit us at our website www.alondrapress.com